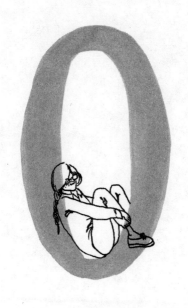

THE
AGONY
OF
BUN
O'KEEFE

THE AGONY OF BUN O'KEEFE

HEATHER SMITH

PENGUIN TEEN CANADA
an imprint of Penguin Random House Canada Young Readers,
a Penguin Random House Company

The following works are referenced in the novel:
The Agony of Jimmy Quinlan, Robert Duncan (writer/producer),
National Film Board, 1978.
Excerpt from "At the Quinte Hotel," from *Poems for All the Annettes*, copyright 1973, 2012
by Al Purdy. Reprinted by permission of House of Anansi Press Inc.
Excerpts from *Horton Hatches the Egg* by Dr. Seuss, Trademark™ and copyright © by
Dr. Seuss Enterprises, L.P. 1940, renewed 1968. Used by permission of Random House
Children's Books, a division of Penguin Random House LLC. All rights reserved.

First published 2017

1 2 3 4 5 6 7 8 9 10 (RRD)

Jacket design by Jennifer Griffiths

Manufactured in the U.S.A.

Library and Archives Canada Cataloguing in Publication

Smith, Heather, 1968-, author
The agony of Bun O'Keefe / Heather Smith.

Issued in print and electronic formats.
ISBN 978-0-14-319865-9 (hardback).—ISBN 978-0-14-319866-6 (epub)

I. Title.

PS8637.M5623A63 2017   jC813'.6   C2016-905832-8
                                               C2016-905833-6

Library of Congress Control Number: 2016952308

We acknowledge the financial support of the Government of Canada through the
Canada Book Fund and that of the Government of Ontario through the Ontario Media
Development Corporation's Ontario Book Initiative. We further acknowledge the support of
the Canada Council for the Arts and the Ontario Arts Council for our publishing program.

ONTARIO ARTS COUNCIL
CONSEIL DES ARTS DE L'ONTARIO

www.penguinrandomhouse.ca

Penguin
Random House
PENGUIN TEEN CANADA

To Kathy Stinson, mentor and friend.
And, always, to Rob.

ONE

She yelled, "Go on! Get out!" So I did. It wasn't easy. The path to the door was filled in again. I tried to keep it clear. But it was like shoveling in a snowstorm. There was only so much I could pile up on either side before it started caving in again. Not that I left the house much.

At one point I had to turn sideways and suck in. I wondered how she did it. She was over three hundred pounds. As I inched forward I saw frozen smiles through a clear plastic bin. Barbie Dolls, $10 As Is.

I knew without looking there'd be some without limbs.

I tripped on a lamp and fell on a bike. She didn't even laugh. The only sound was the tick-tick-tick of the bike's spinning wheel. I watched till it slowed to a stop.

I took one last look at her before I disappeared behind a mountain of junk. She was nestled into a pile of garbage bags, a cup of tea balanced on her chest, and I wondered, how will she get up without me?

Boxes and bags lined the walls. As I squeezed down the hall I said *therianthropy* over and over 'cause I liked the way it bounced in my mouth. It was one of the words I said out loud when I hadn't used my voice in a while. It meant "having the power to turn into an animal." I'd read it in an old anthropology textbook and I thought, Wouldn't it be nice if my mother could turn herself into a hummingbird? That way she could flit in and out through the piles of junk that filled every nook and cranny of the house. It was a nice thought, her being a shape-shifter. Maybe, I decided, that's how I should remember her.

~

I walked down our laneway with my arms crossed over my chest. I had forgotten my jacket. I wouldn't go back for it. Not after the trouble it took me to get out.

I counted Mississippis down the long gravel road. By the time I reached the highway I'd had two coughing fits. She did the trek every day. An empty wagon on the way into town, a full one on the way back. I figured she had exceptional lungs.

At the main road I stuck out my thumb. What I knew about hitchhiking came from *The Texas Chain Saw Massacre*. It came home in a box of VHS tapes. When I told her we

didn't have a player she said, "There she goes, never satis-
fied, always asking for more." When I pointed out that I had
asked for nothing and was simply stating a fact, she didn't
talk to me for days. Months later a VHS player showed up
and I popped in the tape. I watched it on the floor model TV
she'd pulled home on a wooden toboggan. It had a missing
button so I had to change the channel with a pair of pliers.
The screen had fuzzy lines going through it, which made the
movie even scarier. The hitchhiker wanted to kill people. I
had no intentions of killing anyone so I figured there was no
harm in sticking out my thumb on the main road.

I went to St. John's. Seemed as good a place as any. Only
two hours away and easy to disappear into.

~

I figured there were places for people like me, people whose
mother said, "Go on! Get out!" After all, there were places
for people like Jimmy Quinlan. He was in the box with *The
Texas Chain Saw Massacre*. He drank too much alcohol and
lived on the streets of Montreal. Just one of the many "derelict human beings in Canada—living their lives around a
bottle of cheap wine, rubbing alcohol or even, on a bad day,
aftershave lotion."

I watched the documentary so much I'd memorized the
script. Alone in the house I'd recite it. Sometimes I'd say

aftershave lotion, over and over, putting the emphasis on *shave*, just as the narrator had. I'd copy his gravelly voice too. I'd say, "Quinlan's nerves are raw," till I wasn't me anymore; I was a faceless man in the TV.

I walked along Duckworth Street and asked the first person that looked like they might know. I waited till he finished his song.

"Any missions around here?"

"Missions?"

"Yes. Where alcoholics with no homes go."

He smiled. "You're an alcoholic, are you?"

"No. But I have no home."

"Sorry. I don't know of any missions."

"Are you sure?"

"I'm sure."

I must have looked doubtful 'cause he said, "Why are you asking *me*? Do I look like a homeless alcoholic?"

He looked nothing like Jimmy Quinlan or the other derelict human beings. For one thing, he had teeth. But he *was* begging, which is what Jimmy Quinlan did within the first two minutes of the film. He stopped cars and people on the busy streets. *"Bonjour, monsieur! Bonjour, monsieur!"*

"You look like a normal person," I said. "But you *are* begging."

He gathered the loose change from the guitar case in front of him. "I'm not begging. I'm busking."

"So you have a home?"

"I never said that."

"So you *don't* have a home."

He fit his guitar into the guitar-shaped space and squinted at me. "Who are you?"

"Bun O'Keefe."

He snapped the lid shut and hopped to his feet. "First time in the city?"

"Yes."

"How did you get here?"

"Hitchhiked."

"You shouldn't do that."

"Why not? I wasn't going to murder anyone."

He gave me a funny look and headed down a steep hill toward the harbor. He didn't say good-bye so I followed. When he went into a coffee shop, I stood behind him in line, and the girl behind the counter said, "You two together?" and I said, "Yes." She asked me what I'd like to order and I didn't know 'cause I'd never ordered anything before so she suggested tea. I said no in a voice louder than I had meant—I was sick of tea—it's what I drank to keep my stomach from growling. She suggested hot chocolate and I said yes 'cause I hadn't had one since my father left.

My mother called me presumptuous once, after I'd asked her what was for supper. I wondered if I was being that now, so I looked at Busker Boy, but he just nodded at a table and said, "I'll bring it over."

I sat on my hands till he came, then wrapped them around the mug.

He reached into his backpack and pulled out a thick flannel shirt. "When you run away in November, you should wear a coat."

His voice was calm and even, like the narrator of Jimmy Quinlan. It was smoother, though, and softer. All the expression was in his dark brown eyes.

I put my lips to the mug, letting the steam fog my glasses. "I didn't run away. My mother told me to leave. So I did."

"How old are you? Twelve?"

"Fourteen."

I read an article about small talk once. It said if you want to create a bond with your conversation partner you should mirror them, so I said, "How old are you? Twelve?" He laughed. "Twenty-one."

He looked me up and down. "You're small for fourteen."

"Is that bad?"

"Not at all. Look at me."

I did. He was short but thick and bulging with muscles. Stocky would be the word.

"As long as you're strong, that's all that matters. Are you strong?"

I could shift my mother's boxes out of my way when need be. "Yes. I'm strong."

He grinned at me. "Your Smurf shirt kind of threw me off, too."

It could just as easily have been the Bionic Woman or Starsky and Hutch. Both came home in a box called *vintage*. I told my mother that something from a decade earlier couldn't be called vintage, that seventies stuff didn't count. She called me a smartarse and told me to go away.

I pressed rewind. My head whirred.

Your Smurf shirt kind of threw me off, too.

"Are Smurf shirts only for twelve-year-olds?"

"Most girls your age dress way too old, that's all."

"Smurf hats are called Phrygian caps. They symbolize freedom."

He looked at me like I was making things up. But I don't tell lies.

"That coffee stinks."

A gentle laugh. "Who are you?"

"I told you. Bun O'Keefe."

"I like you, Bun O'Keefe."

Once, I stuck a knife in a toaster 'cause my bread was stuck and I felt a jolt. When he said, "I like you," I felt the same way—it wasn't just a surprise, it was a shock that zinged.

"They called me weird the year I went to school. 'Cause I say things that pop in my head."

"You only went to school for one year?"

"Kindergarten. No one said, 'I like you, Bun O'Keefe.'"

He said, "That's sad."

I said, "Is it?"

He stared into his coffee.

I said, "Did you know that if you smile, even when you're not happy, your mood will improve? It's a scientific fact."

The corners of his lips curled upward.

I said, "You look like the Joker from Batman."

I liked his laugh. It fluttered like a leaf on the breeze.

I took a sip of my hot chocolate.

He took a sip of his coffee.

I wondered if he was trying to create a bond.

I said, "Want to know the difference between a real smile and a fake smile?"

"Sure."

"With a real smile the orbicularis oculi muscle contracts and makes wrinkles around your eyes. Has that ever happened to you? I don't think that's ever happened to me."

Lines covered his forehead. I was about to tell him he was contracting his frontalis muscle when he said, "Are you hungry? I can get you a cookie."

"Two please. No ants."

His forehead crinkled even more.

"Raisins," I said. "No raisins."

Alone at the table, I wrapped the flannel shirt tighter

around me and leaned forward, letting the steam from my drink fog my glasses.

~

I sat with him under a sign that said Fred's. He gave me a pair of gloves and a hat from his backpack. They were too big but I didn't say so. He played lots of stuff I recognized from the records that filled our bathtub. Bob Dylan, Queen, The Beatles. Lots of stuff I didn't know, too, and after each one, I'd say, "What was that?" and he'd say, "Violent Femmes" or "The Clash" or "The Cure." I found a paper cup on the ground and held it out to people passing by. I shook it in time with the music until Busker Boy asked me to stop. So I did.

After a song about a guy who plays guitar with spiders from Mars I asked, "So are you homeless?" and he said, "Temporary accommodations. I can't wait to get out."

So I told the passersby. "He lives in temporary accommodations. He can't wait to get out."

Sounded like a good song title. I'd suggest it later.

Three times I emptied the cup into his guitar case.

When he packed up I said, "What now?"

"Home. It's late."

"Yeah, I'm tired too."

He pulled up the hood of his sweatshirt and buttoned up his jean jacket. We walked for ages.

"What's this road called?"

"Water Street."

"It's long."

"We'll be there soon."

I couldn't stop yawning. "Yawning is called oscitation."

He said hmmm to let me know that he heard me. I liked that.

"The average yawn lasts six seconds. I read it in a book."

A man staggered toward us in the opposite direction. Busker Boy grabbed me by the elbow and pulled me across to his other side, near the road.

"Why'd you do that?" I asked.

When the man passed, Busker Boy pulled me back on the inside. "He was drunk."

"Homeless too?"

"Maybe."

It got real quiet as we walked, and I filled the empty space around me the way I usually did—with words. "There are about five thousand Jimmy Quinlans on the streets of Montreal, maybe even more in Toronto and Vancouver. No one dares guess the exact number of derelict human beings in Canada."

He looked at me funny again.

"It's from a documentary."

"And you memorized it?"

"The voice too."

"You should get out more."

"Why?"

"Fresh air is good for you."

"Why?"

"It makes you feel more alive."

As far as I could tell you could be no more "more alive" than you could be "more dead."

I breathed in the cold, salty air. It caught at my throat and made me cough.

"Are you sick?"

"No. Why?"

"You have a cough."

"No, I don't."

We kept walking.

"I wish I could un-read that."

He looked around. "Un-read what?"

"The poster on the pole we just passed."

"What did it say?"

"'An Evening of Edgar Allan Poe: Selected Readings.'"

"What's wrong with that?"

"'The Tell-Tale Heart' came home in a box. I wish I'd never read it. I'll never sleep tonight now."

"How come?"

"Somebody murders somebody else and dismembers the body."

"Maybe you should stick to books about yawns."

"I'm tired. How much longer?"

"Not long."

We walked uphill through a dark park. I heard whispers and grunting and laughter.

"Do you have wooden floorboards in your temporary accommodations?"

He thought a moment. "Yes. Why?"

In "The Tell-Tale Heart," the body was hidden under the floor and the murderer was convinced he could hear his victim's heartbeat through the planks.

"Just wondering."

Under the streetlights ahead, a strip of row houses, each a different color.

"We're here."

We entered the sixth one down, yellow with a blue door.

Six, yellow, blue.

Six, yellow, blue.

Six, yellow, blue.

I had no reason to believe I wouldn't be invited back so I memorized it.

The door opened to a steep staircase. When we got to the top, Busker Boy said, "You okay?" and I said, "Why wouldn't I be?" To our left, there was a sparsely decorated living room overlooking the street. To the right, a kitchen. Busker Boy pointed straight ahead. "Can you handle one more flight?" I said, "Why wouldn't I?" I counted the steps

in my head. At fourteen he said, "You sound pretty wheezy."
I said, "That's just how I breathe."

At the top there was a landing. Around the landing, five
doors. Four were closed, one was open. Busker Boy pointed
to the open one. "Bathroom."

There was a door with a treble clef on it. Seemed fitting.
Except for the sparkles. "Is that yours?"

"No. Mine's over here."

He moved to the door at the back of the house. There
was another small staircase to the right of it. "Attic. Don't
ever go up there." He turned the knob and said come in. So
I did.

It was a small room, containing only a bed, a dresser and
a side table. He grabbed a comforter and pillow out of the
closet and put them on the floor.

"You can have the bed."

My (his) flannel shirt was long. A good nightshirt, I
thought. I peeled off my jeans, put my glasses on the bedside
table and crawled under the covers.

Busker Boy threw his jean jacket on the dresser. "Warm
enough?"

"No."

He took a leather jacket out of the closet and laid it over
me. "Wear this tomorrow."

He took the elastic out of his hair and peeled off his black
T-shirt. A bear-claw necklace hung around his neck.

He folded the comforter in half and got in between the layers.

"Can I ask you a question?"

I didn't know why he was asking permission.

"Okay."

"Is anyone looking for you?"

"No."

"You don't have to tell me why you left."

"She told me to leave."

"I think we both know there's more to the story than that."

Was there?

"Anyway, I'm here if you need to talk."

It took a lot of energy but I lifted my head up. I was hoping he was wrong but there they were—wooden floorboards. I could hear the heartbeat already.

He reached for the lamp between us. "Time to get some sleep."

He was about to pull the chain when I reached out and touched his hand. "Can you leave it on? Till I fall asleep?"

He nodded. "Okay."

A while later I woke up. It was dark. I turned on the light and hung over the side of the bed. I shook Busker Boy by the shoulder.

"What is it?"

"I thought of a good title for a song. 'Temporary Accommodations (I Can't Wait to Get Out).'"

"What?"

"I meant to say it earlier. But I forgot. Use parentheses though, around the last part."

I'd seen it done before on cassette tapes she'd brought home. Like, "Take My Breath Away (Love Theme from *Top Gun*)" and "I Ran (So Far Away)."

He fumbled for the light. "Okay."

I touched his hand. "Can you leave it on? Till I fall asleep?"

He nodded. "Good night, Bun O'Keefe."

TWO

When I woke up he was sitting at the end of my (his) bed with a newspaper.

"Oh. You read."

"You sound surprised."

I did?

"You shouldn't judge a book by its cover, you know."

I pressed rewind.

Oh. You read.

You sound surprised.

Oh. You read.

Oh. You read.

"I was just stating a fact. Not everyone reads. My mother never did. We never had anything to talk about."

He put the paper down. "Sorry."

"About what?"

"Snapping at you. Your mother."

"You didn't snap. And my mother's my mother."

He passed me a bag. "I got you this when I picked up my paper. No ants."

The muffin was warm and the milk was cold. I didn't normally cry but I felt like I could.

He flicked open his paper. "I can read the headlines out loud and we can talk about them if you like."

No one had ever read me anything before. "Okay."

He scanned the page. "Let's see. President Ronald Reagan is accused of selling arms to Iran."

"That means weapons," I said.

"Yes," he said. "I know."

"I found a book once called *A Farewell to Arms*. I wondered if it was about amputees. But it was about war."

Busker Boy's lips curled into a smile. I couldn't see why. There was nothing funny about war.

I changed the subject.

"Ronald Reagan was in a movie with a monkey."

"He was?"

"Yeah. And his nickname is the Gipper. Reagan, not the monkey."

"Hmmm."

"His father called him Dutch, though. 'Cause he looked like a fat little Dutchman."

He laughed. "You should write his biography."

"There already is one. It came home with a toaster oven. The sticker said twenty-five cents."

"Twenty-five cents for a toaster oven? Wow, that's cheap."

"No, I meant the book."

"I know. I was joking."

"Oh."

He kept reading.

"Here's a good one. Mike Tyson won a world boxing title."

"Boxing is also called pugilism."

"How do you know that?"

"It's in the dictionary."

"You read the dictionary?"

"You don't?"

I was surprised. It was the most famous book in the world.

Someone hammered on the door.

Busker Boy peered over the paper. "Someone is pugilizing the door right now."

I was pretty sure that wasn't a word but didn't say so.

He leaned over and twisted the knob. A cloud of smoke puffed in first, then a man that looked like the guy from *The Shining* (which also came home in a box with Jimmy Quinlan). He rolled his cigarette from the middle of his mouth to the left. I wondered if he used his tongue or if it was a trick of the lips. He stared at me and spoke out of the right side of his face. "Who do we have here?"

Busker Boy said, "Nobody." As he walked to the night-
stand he pulled my blankets up around my waist.

The man's cigarette rolled from the left to the right and
back again. Smoke drifted through his nose like a dragon.

Busker Boy took an envelope out of the drawer and
tossed it to the end of the bed.

Dragon Man reached for it but kept his eyes on me.
"Why don't you come to the attic, little one, and tell me a
story?"

I looked at Busker Boy. "I could. I know lots of stories."

Busker Boy walked to the door and shut it in Dragon
Man's face. "Why would you say that?"

"Say what?"

"That you know lots of stories."

"'Cause I do."

He gathered his bedding from the floor. "Don't ever go
up to that man's room. Don't even talk to him."

"Why not?"

"He's not a nice person. Can't you see that?"

I couldn't so I said so.

"You have to be more careful. You can't just talk to
anybody."

"I talked to you. You're nice."

"You didn't even ask my name."

"I knew the names of all twenty-three kids in my kindergarten class. There was no advantage as far as I could tell."

He threw his comforter and pillow into the closet. "Just promise me you'll never go near the landlord."

What I knew about promises came from *Horton Hatches the Egg*. It was a library discard and the pages were tearing away from the spine. I read it until the cover came off. Horton had promised a bird he'd sit on her egg while she went on vacation. He sat through rainstorms and snowstorms and was even caught by hunters who put him in a traveling circus. But through it all he stayed on the egg, saying:

I meant what I said
And I said what I meant.
An elephant's faithful
One hundred per cent!

I'd never made a promise before.
"Okay."
"Okay what?"
"I promise."
"Good. Now, let's go busking."
He pulled on his big black boots. I pulled on my white Keds. She found them for $2.50 at a garage sale. "That there is a pair of premium shoes," she'd said. I pointed out the hole in the big toe. Not that I cared what I wore on my feet, but the use of the word *premium* seemed inappropriate, so I told her. She called me a smartarse and told me to go away.

Sometimes, my mother laughed at me. Once, in a box from the thrift shop, there was a bikini. It looked like the one described in *Starring Sally J. Freedman as Herself*—a halter top with ties around the neck and the back. In the book, a boy untied the girl's top and sang, "tiddly winks, tiddly winks." The whole passage confused me—why did he untie it and what were tiddly winks? I had never been swimming and was never likely to, but I thought I might like to try on this bikini. My mother laughed when she saw me: "Grow some tits."

Busker Boy laughed at me, too, when I put on the leather jacket he'd given me. But his eyes were warm and he said, "You've got some growing to do, Bun O'Keefe." I felt like laughing with him. So I did. Not my usual laugh, the crazy haw-haw-haw I'd perfected from *Planet of the Apes*, but my real one. I hardly recognized it.

Before we left I asked him if he could do my hair like his. He spun me around gently by the shoulders and combed my hair with his fingers. He gathered every strand and wisp loosely at my neck. I closed my eyes. After a few gentle twists and tugs, a long braid hung between my shoulder blades.

He passed me my glasses. "Don't forget these."

When I put them on he said, "I hope you don't mind me saying, but they look way too small for you."

"I don't mind you saying."

I think he might've been waiting for me to say something else but I didn't know what, so I said, "I'm somebody, you know."

"What?"

"You said I was nobody."

"I did?"

He looked up, as if the memory was pinned to the ceiling.

"Oh yeah. I did, didn't I?" He slung his guitar on his back. "I didn't want to introduce you to the landlord, that's all. Of course you're somebody. You're a very special somebody."

I wondered what that meant, to be special.

On our way downstairs, a girl with big eyes came out of the kitchen. She said, "It's my day off but you-know-who's working today," and Busker Boy grinned really big, and I said, "Who's you-know-who?" and Big Eyes said, "I like your hair. It's bleepin' gorgeous."

I was more confused by the *gorgeous* than the *bleepin'*.

She touched it. "A perfect strawberry blonde."

Her hair was a fake orangey-red. Like Cyndi Lauper's on the *She's So Unusual* cassette cover. My mother bought it at a garage sale and when she gave it to me she said, "I thought you could relate," and then she laughed and I didn't know why.

"This is Bun," said Busker Boy. "She's staying awhile."

"Doesn't she have a home to go to?"

"No. That's why she's here."

"No one's missing her?"

"There was nothing in the headlines this morning."

Big Eyes stared at me. "We'll get in trouble, you know, if you've run away from home."

"I didn't run away. My mother told me to leave."

"So your face won't be all over the news tonight?"

"I don't think so," I said. "It should be here where it always is, stuck to the front of my head."

Big Eyes burst out laughing. "Come to my room tonight, Bun. I'll curl your hair."

"Okay. I can tell you a story if you like."

I looked at Busker Boy. He winked so I knew it was okay.

~

On our way downtown we stopped at a candy store. The walls were lined with bins. I read the names out loud. Bottle Caps. SweeTARTS. Airheads. Runts. Sour Patch Kids. Busker Boy handed me a bag.

"How much should I get?"

"As much as you want."

He held the bag open and followed me from bin to bin.

"Why did that girl say 'bleepin''?"

"She wants to swear but can't."

"Why does she want to swear?"

"She's trying to change her image."

THE AGONY OF BUN O'KEEFE

"Why?"

He answered but with his eyes on the checkout.

"Her mother was pressuring her to go into a convent. So she split."

"Split what?"

A girl behind the cash waved to him. He passed me the bag. "Meet you up front."

I read the price per pound sign. I wasn't sure if it was good or bad and wondered what my mother would make of it. He said "as much as you want," so I took one more scoop of Runts and tied off the end.

I laid my bag on the counter and the girl weighed it without looking at me. She had a candy pacifier in her mouth and when she told me the price she pulled it out with a *pop!* Her lips were wet and shiny.

Busker Boy reached for his wallet. "She's with me."

Pop Girl gave me a quick once-over then rang in the sale.

Busker Boy asked if she had plans later.

Pop! "Nope."

"You can come to my place. The landlord has darts and the gang should be home."

Pop! "Wicked."

The door jingled as we left. Busker Boy looked back through the window and so did I. Pop Girl pulled the remaining nugget of candy off with her teeth and threw the plastic ring in the trash.

~

I kept falling asleep on the steps of Atlantic Place. I thought it was Busker Boy's singing, but it must have been his voice in general 'cause I dozed off again at the coffee shop while he chatted to a friend. His voice reminded me of the narrator from the *Hinterland Who's Who* TV spots that came on when I was little. The beaver one was my favorite. "With all the woodcutting that the beaver has to do, it's fortunate that his incisor teeth never stop growing. For a more complete story of the beaver, why not contact the Canadian Wildlife Service." I figured only certain people could be narrators: patient people who could keep the script smooth and calm, people like Busker Boy.

On the long way home I talked about space: how Venus is the hottest planet and footprints on the moon will never disappear 'cause there's no wind to blow them away. I talked out loud till I got out of breath, then I talked in my head instead. I said six, yellow, blue to the rhythm of my feet till the house came into view.

When we got inside Busker Boy said I should have a shower. When I asked why he said, "Because you spent half the day conked out on the steps of Atlantic Place," and I said, "Not exactly, you put your jacket down first," and he said, "You should have a shower anyway," and when I asked why he said, "It's a good idea to shower every day," and I said, "Daily showering dries your skin," and he said, "Good hygiene is important," and I said, "Showering too often removes good bacteria that helps maintain healthy skin," and he said, "You are so frustrating it's no wonder your mother kicked you out!"

Somehow I'd managed to make one of the world's most patient people snap.

"I'm sorry," he said. "I didn't mean that."

"It's okay," I said. "She didn't like my facts either. That's why she said, 'Go on! Get out!'"

"I like your facts. They show how smart you are."

Me? Smart?

"You don't have to take a shower. Not if you don't want to."

I had taken one the day before I left. It was a Tuesday, the only day of the week I left the house. The thirty-minute walk to the RV park was easier than moving boxes out of the shower stall at home.

"I snapped because I'm nervous," he said.

"About what?"

"The girl I was talking to today? She'll be here soon. I'm not sure I'm her type."

"I think you're the nicest person I've ever met."

We both smiled then, big and wide with wrinkles all round our eyes.

"I'm going to have a shower now and then get my hair curled. Okay?"

"Okay."

He passed me a towel. It smelled like a rainbow. I know 'cause I climbed one once in a dream.

"Bun?"

"Yeah?"

"Are you going to smell that towel all day or are you going to take that shower?"

I said, "But it's full of colorful scents."

I was halfway out the door when he said, "Bun? That mother of yours is really missing out."

I was going to say on what, but decided not to say everything that popped in my head.

~

Big Eyes answered her door in a pink crop top and yellow leggings. "Oh good. You're here."

She plugged in her hairdryer and curling iron and pointed to the bed with her brush. "Sit."

Duran Duran stared at me from every angle.

"Who's your favorite?" she asked.

I recognized them from my mother's *People* magazine, the one with Princess Diana on the front. The article was called "A Romp with the Idol Rich." I was more interested in "Malice in the Palace." Apparently, Di was bossing the servants around and dancing the night away without Charles.

"I don't have a favorite."

"You like them all, huh?"

"I don't like any of them."

She put a hand on her hip. "You can't be bleepin' serious."

"I can be. And I am."

"Sorry, but if that's the case, we can't be friends."

I stood up. "Oh. Okay."

"Bun! Sit down. I'm only joking."

She sat behind me cross-legged on the bed. "Let's brush out this gorgeous head of hair."

The bangles on her wrist clinked with each stroke.

I had a kitten once. It showed up in a box marked Fabric Remnants $2.50. It sat on my lap and I stroked its fur. The rumbling beneath my hand drowned out the rumbling in my belly and I felt full, of what I didn't know, but I was both sleepy and content. The kitten was mine, all mine, until a barbell rolled out of a toaster oven that had been placed on a bag of old coat hangers.

There, on Big Eyes's bed, I had that rumbly kitten feeling. My head swayed back in rhythm, and she was humming a song I recognized. I liked the way the bristles tickled my scalp, and if humans could purr, I probably would have.

"Bun?"

"Yeah?"

"I know what it's like, you know. Not getting along with your mother."

"You know my mother?"

She smiled. "What I mean is, I get it. Some bridges can't be rebuilt."

"They can't?"

"Nope. So you won't hear me convincing you to go back."

"I won't?"

"Not a bleepin' chance."

I slipped my fingers in a rip in her comforter and felt the cottony fluff underneath.

"Don't mind the holes. They were going to throw it out at the hotel but Chef brought it home because he knew I didn't have one."

"Who's Chef?"

"He's one of our roommates."

"Is his room the one with the sparkly treble clef?"

"Ha! No. Oh, by the way, you know to stay away from the landlord, right? He's a total creep. If he tries to talk to you, just tell him to bleep off. That's what I do."

I hummed along to the drone of the hairdryer. Big Eyes switched it off. "What's that noise?" I listened all around. "I don't hear anything." She turned it on again. I hummed so low my teeth rattled. "Are you humming?" she shouted. My heart did a flip. "I'll stop if you want." She bent down and whispered in my ear, "Hum away, my darling. I just wondered, that's all."

My darling.

I hummed till my hair was bone dry.

She chattered nonstop as she curled my hair. She talked about Simon Le Bon's bleepin' gorgeous eyes and how the candy store was a great place to work but dangerous if you liked wearing belly shirts.

I could kind of see how Simon Le Bon's eyes might be regarded as nice, but no matter how many times I pressed rewind, I couldn't make the connection between danger and belly shirts.

She leaned in close to curl the hair near my face. She smelled like a baby I'd held at the RV park. Its mother had asked me to hold it while she had a shower. It pulled my hair and drooled on my shoulder but it smelled nice. And so did Big Eyes. So I told her.

She laughed. "I smell like a baby? One with a full diaper or one straight out of the bath?"

"Straight out of the bath."

She put down the iron and took a bottle off her dresser.

"Hold out your wrists."

She pumped the bottle twice on each wrist.

"Love's Baby Soft. Got it for my birthday."

"Happy Birthday."

"It's not today. It was back in August. Before I left."

She rolled a strand of hair onto the curling iron. "Rub your wrists together."

I did.

"Now smell them."

I did that too.

"Like it?"

When I nodded she said, "Watch your head, hon, this is hot."

She released the final curl. I felt different, like I had a new head. She loosened each ringlet with her fingers, then combed them upwards till they went big and frizzy. She told me to close my eyes and when I did, she drowned me in hairspray.

"There. Bleepin' gorgeous."

She stood back. "I gotta say, though. You're awfully pale."

She dabbed a big brush in pink powder and stroked my cheeks. "That's better."

Another step back. "Want some shadow?"

Her eyelids were layered with color, like the rainbow I'd climbed in my dream.

"No thanks."

There was a knock on the front door.

She pulled the plug on the iron. "I'll get it. Meet me in the living room."

"Wait. I was going to tell you a story. While you did my hair."

"Never mind. Next time."

She took a quick look at herself in a full-length mirror, then wrapped herself up in an oversized cardigan.

THREE

On my way to the living room I heard *pssst* from the kitchen.
A guy with a Mohawk held out a spoon.

"Honey-garlic sauce. For wings. Wanna taste?"

It smelled good so I said okay.

"Bun, what are you doing?"

Busker Boy was behind me.

"I'm going to try this guy's sauce."

"Who's *this guy*?"

"I don't know."

"You shouldn't talk to strangers."

"Why not?"

"Because there are some rotten people out there."

"Is he a rotten person?"

"He's fine. But you didn't know that when you said yes
to his sauce."

33

The guy with the Mohawk slopped his spoon back into the pot. "Jesus, you'd think I was pushing drugs."

I couldn't make Big Eyes's danger–belly shirt connection, but I thought maybe the Mohawk guy could be the other roommate.

"Are you Chef?"

"See?" he said. "She does know me. Can she taste my sauce now?"

A sigh. "Go ahead."

Chef held the spoon to my lips. "Careful, it's hot."

Once, my mother brought home fresh strawberry jam that a farmer was selling at a flea market. She only gave me one spoonful, but it turned into hundreds 'cause I never forgot the taste and was able to imagine it whenever I wanted.

"Well?"

"It's food."

Chef said, "No need to be sarcastic," and Busker Boy said, "I don't think she does sarcasm," and I said, "I mean real food, like, so real my mouth is going to remember it for a long time," and Chef said, "Who are you?" and I said, "Bun O'Keefe," and he said, "I think we're going to be great friends, Bun O'Keefe."

~

34

There was a beanbag chair in a nook that I figured was meant for a TV 'cause of all the outlets. I thought it was cozy but Busker Boy pulled me out and said, "Join the party, Bun."

Everyone had a bottle of something except Busker Boy, and when Pop Girl asked why, he said, "I don't drink."

I read a poem once called "A Dream Pang." In it, a guy hides in the woods watching his lover decide whether to follow his footsteps into the forest. He says, "And the sweet pang it cost me not to call." I wasn't sure what a pang was so I looked it up. I'd never felt a sudden feeling of emotional distress before—until Pop Girl looked at Busker Boy and said, "You don't drink? That's ironic." It wasn't 'cause of her words, which made no sense to me, but 'cause of the look on Busker Boy's face when she said them. He'd felt a pang, I could tell, and his pang caused mine.

Big Eyes changed the subject. "What do you guys think of Bun's hair?"

"It looks nice," Busker Boy said. "Not sure about that pink stuff on her cheeks though. You've hidden her freckles."

"Yeah, but she really needed it. She's as white as a bleepin' ghost. No offense, Bun."

Pop Girl suggested they focus less on my hair and makeup and more on the fact that my glasses looked like they'd fit a five-year-old, and I said, "That's when I got them," and they said, "You haven't had new glasses since you were five?" and I said, "No, 'cause that's when my dad left," and they said, "What about your mother?" and I said, "What about her?"

Chef passed me a bottle. "For what it's worth, I think you look just fine."

"Don't give her that," said Busker Boy.

"Why not?"

"She's too young."

"How old is she?" asked Chef.

"Fourteen."

"It's one beer," said Pop Girl. "What's the problem?"

"She's a *young* fourteen."

I wasn't sure what that meant. Fourteen was fourteen.

I passed it back. "Lord Byron said, 'A woman should never be seen eating or drinking, unless it be lobster salad and Champagne, the only true feminine and becoming viands.' *Viands* means 'food.' I looked it up."

Big Eyes said, "She sounds like an old fourteen to me."

Pop Girl asked what language I was speaking. I said English.

Busker Boy picked up his guitar. "Any requests?"

I said "Footloose" but not 'cause I wanted to hear it.

Busker Boy laughed. "Sorry. Not my style."

"It wasn't a request," said Big Eyes. "I was humming it earlier and it just popped in her head."

It was the first time someone knew what I meant. And then I went and ruined it.

"*Footloose* came home in the box with Jimmy Quinlan."

I wasn't good at reading faces, but blank was easy.

Busker Boy strummed his guitar. "Chef? Anything you'd like to hear?"

Chef grinned. "You know the one."

Busker Boy smirked. "Do I?"

"Just play the damn song."

"What song?"

Once, I found a bag of golf balls and a package of Crayola markers in the same box from the thrift shop, so I did what came naturally and colored in all the ball dimples. My mother called me mischievous. I was too little to know what that meant so I looked it up. One of the entries was "naughty," which seemed fitting, but it also said "playfully annoying," and I wished I knew how to add the playfully to the annoying 'cause I only ever managed to be the latter. But Busker Boy, he knew how it was done. He grinned at Chef with shiny eyes and said, "This song you speak of, was it written by Van Morrison?"

Chef sighed. "Yes."

"But recorded by Art Garfunkel?"

"Stop screwing around and play."

"Shall I sing it as Van . . ."

Strum, strum, strum.

"Or Art?"

Chef said, "As yourself, please," and I was glad 'cause we had Art Garfunkel and Van Morrison on eight-track and out of the three Busker Boy was best.

He belted it out.

Chef joined in with the la-la-las and na-na-nas, and when it was over he said, "Best song ever," and passed around a skinny cigarette. Pop Girl breathed it in for a long time before giving it to Busker Boy who passed it on to Big Eyes who barely touched it to her lips but said, "Hot bleep, this bleep is bleepin' good." When it came to me Busker Boy shook his head, so I gave it back to Chef who shared it with Pop Girl, and together they smoked it till it was gone. Busker Boy sang a song about words flowing out like endless rain into a paper cup and his voice was making me sleepy, so I was glad when Chef brought out the food 'cause his honey-garlic wings woke me up. There were tortilla chips with toppings too, and I ate loads and soon I had that rumbly kitten feeling—I was full of something good and it wasn't just the viands on the table.

Chef told me that goat cheese added interest to the typical nacho platter and a few drops of sriracha gave it depth of flavor. Pop Girl took a chip and said, "Mmmm. Spicy. I like things hot." She looked at Busker Boy when she said hot. I wasn't sure why.

I said, "I think the appropriate word would be *spicy*, rather than *hot*. *Hot* refers to temperature and *spicy* refers to flavor. Although, there is something called the Scoville scale. It measures the heat of spicy foods in Scoville heat units. Maybe *pungency* would be a better word 'cause it can't be mistaken for temperature. Scotch bonnet peppers have three hundred and fifty thousand SHU."

Chef's eyelids were heavy. "That's rad, man. How do you know this shit?"

"*Shit* is the 'appropriate' word," said Pop Girl, but then she laughed and said, "Just kidding."

"Bun knows lots of facts," said Busker Boy. "Don't you, Bun?"

The way he said it, it was like he was proud.

"I know lots of stories too," I said. "I have one about spicy food. If you want to hear it."

"Go for it," said Chef.

I settled into the beanbag chair. "Okay. So a king named Solomon invited the Queen of Sheba to his place for an overnight visit. He offered her a feast but made the food really spicy on purpose. At bedtime she asked him to not force himself on her while she slept, and he said only if you don't steal from me, and she thought, Why would I steal from you? Later, she woke up thirsty 'cause of the spicy food, so she took a drink of water from a glass that was left by her bed. Suddenly Solomon appeared and said that she'd broken her promise so she had no choice but to have sex with him."

"How is drinking water stealing?" asked Big Eyes.

"Solomon said that water was the most valuable of all his possessions."

"What a creep," said Pop Girl. "He basically raped her."

"Yeah, but the fact is, she broke the promise," I said. "So she got what she deserved."

"What a terrible thing to say," said Busker Boy.

It was just like with my mother. The only way I knew I'd said something wrong was not by the words themselves but by the reaction to them.

"He set a deliberate trap," said Big Eyes. "Why would you put the blame on her?"

I shrugged.

"I don't think you should be reading stories like that," said Busker Boy, "let alone re-telling them as some sort of lighthearted tale."

I wondered what Horton would make of the Queen of Sheba.

"And why you'd conclude that 'she got what she deserved' is beyond me," he said. "I actually find it kind of disturbing."

"Okay," said Chef. "You don't need to beat a dead horse. I think she gets it now."

As far as I could tell the only thing that was disturbing was the idea of someone beating a dead horse. What would be the point?

It took a while for the mood to get back to where it was, but soon everyone was singing and chatting like normal and I didn't speak, not 'cause I was trying to stay out of trouble but 'cause I was doing a lot of rewinding in my head.

The downstairs door opened and I wondered if it was Dragon Man, but a woman appeared in the living room. She wore a tight, silky gown with feather trim on the sleeves. Her hair was jet black and straight, and as she walked in she flicked it off her shoulders. Busker Boy picked up his guitar and together they sang "I Got You Babe," and I said, "Sonny and Cher," 'cause I'd seen it on reruns. The tall, skinny lady said, "Not Sonny, just Cher," and she shook my hand and said, "Who are you?" and I said, "Bun O'Keefe." She said, "Short for Bernice, right? I had an Aunt Bun once; she was a nasty old bag," and I said, "How come you look like a woman but sound like a man?" Pop Girl said I was rude but Busker Boy said, "She means no harm," and I was glad 'cause I didn't want him to beat a dead horse again.

~

At midnight Busker Boy said, "Off to bed, Bun," and I said, "Okay," but I didn't move 'cause I was sunk into the beanbag chair, heavy, deep and warm. "Go on," he said and I got a funny feeling, like he might add, "Get out," so I got up quick and stumbled out the door. "Bun," he said, "slow down," but I didn't 'cause if he added, "Get out," I wasn't sure where I'd go—there were no missions around here. He caught up to me on the stairs. "Bun, stop." I paused on the second last step. "I'll be up soon, okay?"

I went to bed and stared at the wall, wondering when "soon" would be.

Their voices came through a vent in the floor. I was a problem, a puzzle, a quagmire, a plague. But Pop Girl had all the answers. Police, social services, a bus ticket home.

When Busker Boy came to bed I said, "I like it here." He said, "I know what it's like to miss someone you love." I said, "She's not missing me." He said, "Tell me, Bun, what was it like?" I thought for a full five minutes. "It was like being a skeleton. A frame with nothing inside."

He touched my arm, rubbed the flannel between his fingers. "Want me to get you a proper pair of pajamas?"

"No. I like this shirt."

He got into his bed on the floor. "Will I wait for you to fall asleep before turning out the light?"

I thought of the floorboards and said yes.

I closed my eyes, listened to the sound of his breath. It flowed out easy, no whistles or sighs.

I said, "Are you asleep?"

"Not yet. Why?"

"I have a question."

"Okay. What is it?"

"Does Cher live in the sparkly treble clef room?"

Busker Boy laughed. "How'd you guess?"

~

THE AGONY OF BUN O'KEEFE

In the morning he was at the end of the bed reading his paper.

"Here."

"What is it?"

"Herbal tea. For your cough."

"What cough?"

"You're so used to it you don't even hear it."

I took a sip. "Ew."

"You were very restless last night."

I was?

"It's no surprise. You've been through a lot."

I have?

"I'm sorry this place isn't much."

There was a crack in the wall at the end of my (his) bed. I liked that crack. I couldn't see the walls at home.

"Read me something?"

"Chef wants to see you in the kitchen first. Take your tea."

He passed me my jeans as I walked to the door. "Put these on." So I did.

Chef wasn't in the kitchen, but Cher was. She was wearing jeans too, and her hair wasn't long and black anymore, but spikey and blonde. It looked like her eyelashes had shrunk too.

"Hello, Bun O'Keefe, my darling."

"Are you a *he* today?"

"Chris by day. Cher by night. Well, not always. Cher has a mind of her own."

"Where's Chef?"

"Gone to work. He left you these."

They looked like pancakes from the Aunt Jemima commercial only fatter. Next to the plate was a note. "Hope your mouth remembers these too."

I poked one with my finger.

"Don't tell me you've never seen a touton before."

I wasn't sure how to answer. Did he want me to tell him or not?

"Where've you been living, my ducky? Under a rock?"

He poured some molasses on my plate.

"Chef made the dough fresh this morning. Fried it up just before he left for work. It's still warm."

He took my fork and knife and cut up my food. "Jesus, Mary and Joseph, would you like me to chew it up for you too?"

"That wouldn't be very hygienic."

"No. It wouldn't. So eat up, for the love of God."

I wasn't religious. But I ate it anyway.

He poured himself a coffee. "I wasn't offended by what you said last night. We drag queens aren't always known for our femininity. Especially in the voice department."

"What's a drag queen?"

"A man who likes to perform as a woman."

"Like Divine," I said, and I started to sing "You Think You're a Man." Chris used my fork as a microphone and joined in.

"Your voice is way more feminine than Divine's," I said, and then I did my best impersonation of her tough, gruff voice.

Chris doubled over laughing. "Oh my God. That is seriously the best impression I've ever heard. I'm speechless, truly speechless."

I was confused. "How can you be speechless when you just said a whole bunch of words?"

He wiped his eyes. "You're a friggin' riot, Bun O'Keefe."

As far as I knew a riot was a violent, chaotic situation. I wished I had a dictionary to see if there was an alternate entry.

"I'd never seen a man dressed as a woman before," I said. "Not until that Divine video. I felt bad for her at first, 'cause she wasn't doing a very good job. Her lipstick was way outside the lines and you could tell she was wearing a wig. But last night, your lipstick was perfect and your hair was so straight it looked like you ironed it."

He fluttered his eyelashes at me. "Why thank you, Bun. It's nice to know that *somebody* appreciates the artistry of the drag queen. Most people think we're from another planet."

"Well those people aren't very smart. There's no evidence of life on other planets."

"No, my darling, what I mean is, they think we're different, like strange alien beings."

"And being different is enough to not like someone?"

"Sadly, yes."

"If strange alien beings *did* exist, they might have something to teach us humans. But then we'd never know, would we? Not if people didn't bother to get to know them. Is that sad?"

I asked 'cause I wasn't sure. But Chris didn't answer. I guess he was too speechless to say he was speechless.

~

Busker Boy said he had to run errands so I spent the morning with Chris. We hung out in his room, which I liked 'cause it had a canopy bed, and I said, "Wow, you're like a queen," and he said, "You got that right, honey." He had licorice in his bedside table and he said, "Let's rot our teeth," and even though I didn't want cavities I ate six ropes. He told me he performed at a place called Priscilla's and he showed me all his gowns.

"Want a sneak peek of my new number?"

"Okay."

He was singing "Gypsys, Tramps & Thieves" when Big Eyes walked in with a shopping bag. "I'm supposed to give you this."

I pulled out seven pairs of Wonder Woman underwear with matching undershirts, two long-sleeved shirts, a stick of deodorant, a toothbrush, a bottle of Suave shampoo with Smurfette on the label and five pairs of socks.

Chris rubbed a shirt sleeve between his fingers. "Polyester. Pffft. He's got the face of a model but he knows nothing about fashion."

Big Eyes passed me a small paper bag. "And these."

I remembered the song from the commercial. "All the good times, all the growing, all the laughter and the tears, these are the Stayfree years."

I passed them back. "I don't need these."

"Well maybe not right this minute, ducky," said Chris, "but you wouldn't want to be caught out."

"Caught out where?"

Busker Boy appeared in the doorway. I waved the sanitary napkins at him. "I don't need these."

I had heard the expression "A deer in the headlights" before but could never quite picture it. Till now.

"I didn't know you were here. I just came for the hair-dryer."

"Underoos?" said Chris. "She's not five."

"They come in size twelve to fourteen so I figured they were okay."

"I don't care what size they come in. Have you seen the commercials? They're for kids."

"She *is* a kid."

"How can you say that? You just bought her Stayfree!"

"I'm sure they're fine," said Big Eyes. "Everyone likes Wonder Woman, right, Bun?"

Busker Boy rubbed his temples like he was an Advil commercial. "Can I just have the hairdryer? I don't want to deal with this."

"Deal with what?" I asked.

"Girl issues."

"What's wrong with girl issues?"

"They're embarrassing."

"For who?"

Chris leaned back on his pillow, his eyes moving back and forth like he was watching a tennis match. I tossed the package to Busker Boy. "Maybe you can get a refund."

He tossed them back. "Keep them. You'll need them."

"Why would I?"

"Because, you know, cycles . . . and stuff."

"I don't have cycles . . . and stuff."

"Can I say something?" said Chris. "This is officially the best conversation ever."

"Wait now," said Big Eyes. "You haven't had a period yet?"

"I thought I had one once. When I was twelve. My *Merck Manual* said another one would come in twenty-eight days. It never did."

"You owned a *Merck Manual*?" said Chris.

"Twelfth edition."

"That's not bleepin' normal," said Big Eyes.

I couldn't see why. "How is reading a medical encyclopedia abnormal?"

"Not the book, the disappearing period."

"I told my mother about it. She said I should be happy and to stop complaining."

"Wait now," said Busker Boy. "Let's rewind."

He did that too?

"What do you mean, *not normal?*" he asked Big Eyes.

Big Eyes leaned into him and whispered, "She could have a bleepin' tumor on her bleepin' thyroid."

Chris rolled his eyes. "And they call *me* a drama queen."

I touched my neck 'cause I knew that's where the thyroid is. "I never considered a tumor," I said. "I just figured I was born without a uterus."

"Oh for God's sake," said Chris. "If you had a period, you have a friggin' uterus."

"I said I *thought* I had a period. Looking back, I probably imagined it 'cause I'd just read *Are You There God? It's Me, Margaret.* That girl was obsessed with periods."

"I don't believe it," said Big Eyes. "No bleepin' uterus?"

Busker Boy's eyes were wide. "Is that even possible?"

"Yup. I looked it up. No uterus, no Stayfree."

"Someone needs to get this girl to the bleepin' doctor. ASAP."

Chris pulled my hand off my neck. "Go get dressed, Bun."

"Wait," said Busker Boy. "She doesn't have a health card and—"

"I'm not taking her to the bloody doctor."

"Where are you going?"

"Shopping. Polyester? Please."

~

He bought me a pair of jeans at the Avalon Mall. "Jordache. Can you feel the difference?"

"Between what?"

"Those and your old ones."

I couldn't so I said so.

"You've got a lot to learn about quality, my ducky."

We walked past a jewelry store. "Want your ears pierced?"

"No."

We walked past a salon. "Want your nails done?"

"No."

"Hair?"

"No."

"Is there *anything* you'd like?"

"A dictionary."

"Good God. Anything else?"

"Something warm."

"Like what?"

"A sweater."

"You're too practical, Bun O'Keefe."

"I'm not practical, I'm cold."

"How cold?"

"Freezing."

"All the time?"

"All the time."

He stared at me for a moment.

"Fine. We'll get a sweatshirt. But I'm choosing it."

It was oversized and said "Frankie Says Relax."

The bus home was a different number. "Where are we going?"

"Somewhere I don't want to go."

"Then why are we going?"

He put his arm around me. "Because I like you, Bun O'Keefe. That's why."

The street sign said Winter Place and the houses were big. Chris stood in front of a white one with black trim and took a deep breath. The bell was a melody. The Westminster Chimes. It was the same tune used in George Harrison's "Ding Dong, Ding Dong" that we had on eight-track at home.

The door opened.

"Hello, Dad."

The floors were dark wood and shiny. We sat on a love-seat in a sunny room. Dad paced in front of us.

"Haven't seen you in months. And now this. You're not sick, are you?"

"I'm fine."

"Then what do you need? Money?"

"Advice."

"I gave you advice years ago: get a girlfriend."

Chris stood up. "This was a mistake."

"If you're a drag queen," I asked, "and you have a girlfriend, does that make you a lesbian?"

Dad had big, bushy eyebrows that covered his eyes when he frowned. "Who are you?"

"Bun O'Keefe."

"No. I mean. Who *are* you?"

"She's a friend," said Chris.

"She's very young."

"Yes," said Chris. "Vulnerable too."

"She's not pregnant, is she?"

I said, "You can't get pregnant without a uterus."

Dad frowned at me. "You don't have a uterus?"

"Do me a favor, Bun," said Chris. "Stop talking."

"Well?" said Dad. "What's the problem?"

"She's fourteen," said Chris. "Suffers from amenorrhea. I'm not sure why."

Dad looked me up and down. "Slightly delayed pubertal

development. But I wouldn't worry. Not till she's sixteen."

"She thinks she had a period once. Two years ago."

Dad raised an eyebrow. "So you're thinking secondary amenorrhea?"

Chris nodded. "She's cold all the time. Pale too."

Dad leaned over and pulled my bottom eyelid down. He sat next to me on the loveseat. "How's your diet?"

"I'm not on one."

He looked at Chris. "Saucy little thing, isn't she?"

"He means do you eat well," said Chris. "You know, healthy food? Fruit and veg?"

There had been a Canada's Food Guide magnet on the fridge at home. I had tried to convince myself that a handful of Cheezies was a serving of dairy and a mouthful of Cherry Coke was a fruit.

"Well?" said Dad. "How is your diet?"

My mother didn't follow the guide at all. The last thing I wanted was to be like her.

I said, "The *meat and alternative* category was pretty easy. Two servings a day. I could make a can of Vienna sausages last three days. Except there were seven in a tin. The last one was half a serving so I just threw it out."

Dad looked at Chris. "What is she rambling about?"

"The Canada Food Guide by the sounds of it."

"I found it in a bag of old shoes," I said. "There was a sun on it, smiling and licking its lips. There was a chicken and a fish with their heads still on. It said, 'Eat a variety of foods from each group every day,' but my mother said, 'What are we? Hippies?'"

"So what did you eat?" asked Dad.

"Saltines, mostly."

"That's not very healthy," said Chris.

"Yeah, but they're a bread product. I'd have them with Kraft Singles. That's two food groups in one snack."

Dad and Chris looked at each other.

I said, "I read this quote once, 'One should eat to live, not live to eat.' If that's true, then my mother's been doing it wrong, and I've been doing it right."

Chris looked confused. "Your mother lived to eat saltines and crappy cheese?"

"No. She ate doughnuts and chips and fast food burgers."

"And you didn't?" asked Dad.

"I tried not to," I said. "They're not on the guide."

Dad turned to face me. "You're an odd little thing, aren't you?"

He took my wrist in his hand and looked to the ceiling. He looked in my eyes and my ears and my throat. He listened to my heart.

"So," said Chris. "What do you think?"

"Take her home and fatten her up. She's as thin as a rail. Low body fat is often the culprit in these cases. Get some iron supplements too. No need for further exploration. Not at this stage."

"One more thing."

"Yes?"

"Do you have a spirometer in your office? She has a wheeze."

Dad left the room and came back with a machine. He told me to take a big breath and blow it out into a tube. After a few tries he said, "Asthmatic. Take her to a clinic. They'll prescribe her an inhaler."

"I can't," said Chris. "She's kind of under the radar right now."

Dad said, "You're going to get yourself into a whole heap of trouble."

"You make it sound like I'm harboring a fugitive."

"You are."

"She's not a criminal."

"But she's a runaway."

"I'm not a runaway," I said. "She told me to leave."

Chris stood up. "Time to go, Bun."

Dad walked us to the door.

"You still have what it takes, Christopher. It's not too late to make your mother proud."

"Good-bye, Dad."

~

On the bus ride home I said, "How do you make dead people proud?"

"Good God, Bun. What are you going on about now?"

"He said, 'It's not too late to make your mother proud.' But your mother's dead."

"How do you know?"

"I saw a silver urn over the fireplace that said Rest in Peace. I figured it was your mother's ashes."

"Well done, Sherlock."

"Well? How do you make a dead person proud?"

"I guess you just try to be the best person you can be as a tribute to them."

"Oh. Well in that case, she's already proud. You're one of the best people I know."

"She's not proud, Bun. And she never will be."

"How do you know?"

"Because she died of disappointment."

"She did?"

"Yup. And nothing I do will ever change that."

"Oh, well. She's dead now so I guess it doesn't really matter."

"Gee, Bun. You really know how to cheer a guy up."

I pointed out the window. "Look, the sign on that church says, You Can't Stop, Drop and Roll in Hell."

Chris laughed. "I'd better bring my fire extinguisher."

FOUR

Busker Boy and Pop Girl were in my (his) bed when I got home.

"Jesus," said Busker Boy, pulling up the covers. "You scared me."

I showed them my new sweatshirt and jeans.

Busker Boy said, "Nice." Pop Girl said, "Can you leave now?"

"Give us a few minutes, okay, Bun?"

"Chris took me to see his father and I think they're going to make my period start."

Busker Boy's forehead crinkled. "What?"

"He bought me iron pills too. 'Cause my iron is low. He can tell you all about it. Want me to get him?"

"No," said Pop Girl. "Just go."

So I did. I sat outside the door with the dictionary

Chris had bought me and went to the *r*'s. *Riot: someone or something that is very funny.* Funny was better than violent, I supposed.

I flipped to the *s*'s. *Special: different from what is normal or usual; unusual in a good way.*

I hoped that if Busker Boy's definition of *special* was "unusual," he'd add "in a good way" too.

~

I got tired of waiting for Busker Boy and Pop Girl to finish whatever it was they were doing so I went to the living room. Cher was doing her makeup and Big Eyes was spiking Chef's Mohawk.

"Have fun shopping at the mall?" asked Chef.

"No."

Cher snorted. "That's the last time I take you anywhere."

"I had a good time," I said. "But not 'cause of the shopping."

"What's wrong with shopping?" asked Big Eyes.

I sunk into the beanbag chair. "Everything."

Cher waved her mascara wand at me. "If shopping is wrong, my ducky, then I don't want to be right."

Big Eyes laughed. "Me neither."

"All my mother did was shop. She took me with her once. It was boring."

I hated being squashed in her rickety old wagon surrounded by junk. She only took me 'cause my dad left and I was too young to be left home alone. I started hiding when she was getting ready to leave. She'd look for me for a bit, but eventually she'd just go without me. Sometimes, while she was gone, I got scared. Like the time there was thunder that sounded like bombs. It didn't matter that she wasn't there. I'd have hid in the attic anyway.

Busker Boy joined the rest of us in the living room. Pop Girl hung off him the way baby orangutans hang off their mothers except her feet touched the ground.

Cher zipped up her makeup bag. "Good. Everyone's here."

She filled them in on our visit to Winter Place. She told them about the iron and the low body fat and said, "Basically, what this girl needs is some TLC."

Big Eyes smiled at me. "I think we can manage that."

Chef said he'd come up with some iron-rich recipes.

Pop Girl said, "What's the big deal? Aren't some girls just late bloomers?" and Cher said, "And where did you get your PhD? My father got his at McGill."

"She's only asking," said Busker Boy.

Pop Girl gave me a look that gave me a pang.

Cher said she had to go or she'd be late for work. "One more thing, we need to keep the dust level down in this house. She's got asthma."

"What do you mean, *asthma?*" asked Busker Boy.

"Don't get your knickers in a knot," said Cher, as she slipped into her heels. "It's a common condition. She'll live."

I was glad to hear that.

As Cher passed, Busker Boy grabbed her hand. "Thanks. Going to your dad's couldn't have been easy."

Cher stooped down and put her cheek out. "Plant one there and we're even."

Busker Boy laughed and gave her a kiss.

Before Cher left I said, "Are you still going to take me places?"

"What are you talking about, my ducky?"

"You said today was the last time."

"You need to learn to take a joke, Bun O'Keefe. You know I'd take you anywhere."

~

One of the things I liked about living with Busker Boy was how we ate meals together and at regular times. We were like the Huxtables from *The Cosby Show*—only white and not related and poorer. Chef did most of the cooking and after the visit to Chris's dad he made dishes like beef carbonnade, Indian spiced red lentil soup, potato and spinach frittata. I liked not having to think about the Canada's Food Guide. Chef did all the thinking for me. He said, "You'll have an army of red blood cells marching through your blood in no time."

I liked to help Chef cook, and while we chopped and sautéed, he told me that his job as a dishwasher at the Newfoundland Hotel was temporary and someday he'd cook for kings and queens. He asked me, "What kind of meals did your mom cook for you?" and I said, "My mother didn't cook," and he said, "Then what did you eat?" I said, "Whatever stopped my stomach growling."

One night, after a bowl of hearty vegetable soup, Busker Boy said I had color in my cheeks. He congratulated Chef and told Big Eyes there was no need to put that pink stuff on my face anymore. She told him to bleep off.

~

I opened my eyes. "Read me something?"

He straightened his paper with a snap. "Elie Wiesel won the Nobel Peace Prize."

"Who's that?"

"*You* don't know?"

I shook my head.

"Oh, how the mighty have fallen."

"Book of Samuel."

"What?"

"'How the mighty have fallen.' It's from the Bible."

He didn't say anything, he just stared at me, and all of a sudden I got a panicky feeling like something bad was going to happen, so I said, "Was I being frustrating?" and he said, "Of course you weren't, I was just thinking," and I said, "About what?" and he said, "How you're smart in some ways, but not in others," and then he said, "No offense," and I said, "None taken."

He nodded at the paper. "Want me to keep reading?"

I sat up and pulled the comforter up around my waist. It looked like the one from Big Eyes's bed. "Where did this come from?"

"Another reject from the hotel. It must be warm because you had a good night's sleep. You barely fidgeted at all."

"I fidget?"

"Not as bad as when you first moved in."

"I moved in?"

He laughed. "Looks that way."

"Why are these accommodations temporary?"

"I'm not too fond of them, that's all."

"I like it here. Everyone's really nice."

"Not everyone. Now, shall I continue reading?"

"Okay."

"So, the Nobel Committee says that Wiesel is a messenger to mankind. They say: 'His message is based on his own personal experience of total humiliation and of the utter contempt for humanity shown in Hitler's death camps.'"

"I don't normally cry but I did when I read Anne Frank's diary."

"This guy wrote a book called *Night*. It's about his experience in a concentration camp."

"I'd like to read that."

"I'm not sure I would. Sounds like a tough read."

Sometimes, alone in my house, I'd scan random books, looking for a passage that would jolt me out of my numbness, something that would make my stomach twist and tears well up in my eyes. I rarely found it.

He folded the paper shut. "Time to go busking."

On the way downtown he told me it was Pop Girl's birthday.

"Chef's baking a cake."

I never knew how to respond to statements. Questions were easy. If nothing else you could say, "I don't know." Statements were trickier so I just said, "Hmmm."

"You don't like her, do you?"

"She's never offered to curl my hair, but she's okay, I guess."

"She's a bit cold, at first, a bit icy. But she's warm once you get to know her. When it's just the two of us things are great. Not that I don't want you around or anything," he added. "I didn't mean that. I'd actually like you to get to know her better."

"I'll try."

We made more money than usual in front of Atlantic Place. I thought of Anne Frank and people said, "Poor little thing" and "Here ya go, my ducky." The cup filled up fast.

~

Dragon Man was sitting on the top of the stairs with a bottle that said Jim Beam.

"Thought it was darts night," said Busker Boy.

"It is. Having a tipple before I go."

Busker Boy put me in front of him, hands on my hips, and pushed me past Dragon Man. Dragon Man caught my wrist. "Sit on my lap and tell me a story."

Busker Boy pushed him away. "Get your hands off her."

Dragon Man laughed. "Simmer down, Tonto!"

I turned around. "That's inappropriate."

Dragon Man squinted. "You talking to me?"

"Tonto was an American Indian," I said. "Not Innu."

"A redskin's a redskin."

"Not true," I said. "There are lots of different American Indian tribes . . . Iroquois . . . Cree . . . Apache . . ."

Dragon Man's eyes were slits. "You're a real little know-it-all, aren't you?"

I could have gone on, about the different languages and customs. I wanted to tell him that the actor who played Tonto in *The Lone Ranger* was actually a Mohawk from Canada, not 'cause it was important but 'cause it was an interesting fact, but Busker Boy pulled me away.

We went into the kitchen, where Chef was making Pop Girl's cake.

Busker Boy sat me on a chair and said, "You never told me I was Aboriginal."

"You mean you didn't know?"

"Ha!" said Chef, passing me a beater of icing. "She told a joke."

"She doesn't do jokes," said Busker Boy. "And what I mean is, you never said that you knew I was Aboriginal."

"Why would I?"

"Most people comment."

"Why?"

"They just do."

"Does it matter?"

"No."

"That's why I didn't comment."

"How'd you know I was Innu?"

"Bear claws are symbols of Aboriginal culture."

He touched his necklace. "That's it?"

I grinned in a playfully annoying way. "And I'd asked Chris when I moved in."

Busker Boy grinned back at me. "You moved in?"

I answered with a mouthful of icing. "Looks that way."

Busker Boy laughed and took the beater away. "Enough junk. Go take your iron pill."

~

Chef let me help decorate the cake. He gave me a piping bag and with his hands over mine we made flowers around the border and in the center we wrote *Happy Birthday*.

"When's *your* birthday, Bun?"

"The real one or the fake one?"

"What do you mean?"

"I don't remember the real one 'cause I lost my birth certificate."

"You mean you don't celebrate your birthday with your family?"

"Not since my dad left."

He put a piece of wax paper on the table. "Here, you can practice making flowers with the leftover icing."

He sat next to me.

"So when's your fake one?"

"August sixteenth. The anniversary of Elvis Presley's death."

"I didn't know you were an Elvis fan."

"I'm not. But my mother is. When she plays 'Love Me Tender' and lights a candle, I know that's the day to say, Happy Birthday, Bun O'Keefe."

My flowers were blobs. "I'm not good at this."

"It takes practice. Don't worry, you'll get it."

I kept trying.

"What's TLC?"

"You don't know what TLC is?"

I shook my head.

He put his hand over mine again and piped a perfect flower. "TLC is Tender Loving Care."

He changed the tip. "Try the star."

My stars were stars. "I'm doing it."

"Well done, Sally Lunn."

"Who's Sally Lunn?"

He laughed. "It's a bun. From England. We made them at school today."

"You go to school?"

"Culinary school. You'd get an A Plus for these stars."

"Does the Sally Lunn bun taste nice?"

"It's lovely—part bread, part cake. Like a light brioche."

I thought a brioche was a pin for a lady's blouse.

He switched the star for a leaf. "Give these a try."

My leaves were blobs but he said he'd give me a B.

He added more icing to the bag. "Bun, are you happy?"

"I never really thought about it."

He took the bag and piped my name in fancy letters. "I think about it all the time."

I said, "Have you ever smelled a rainbow?"

He laughed. "Can't say that I have. You?"

"Once, in a dream."

"What did it smell like?"

"Crayons."

"Interesting."

"I climbed it too," I said. "Sat on the top for ages."

"Did you slide down the side to get off?"

"Yes," I said. "How did you know?"

He smiled. "Lucky guess."

"It was a good dream," I said. "Want to borrow it?"

"What?"

"Borrow it. For when you're not sure if you're happy or not."

Chef cleared his throat. "Thank you, Bun. I'd love to."

I said, "Careful on your way up. The red is super slippery."

~

I only remember one gift. It was a red-and-yellow car that you sat in and moved with your feet. I'd go from the living room, to the hall, through the kitchen, and back again. There was room to do that back then. Dad kept the junk neat.

My mother made a cake. She stuck a Barbie waist high in the middle of it. Her skirt was chocolate with pink icing.

It tasted like magic.

They sang "Happy Birthday," told me to make a wish.

I think they might have loved me then.

My father used to sing a song about love being strange and how once you get it you never want to quit.

He was right. Love *is* strange.

But the second part, that was wrong.

People quit all the time.

I never tasted magic again.

~

Before the party, Big Eyes called me into her room. "I have something for you."

She passed me a bag of clothes. "I snuck in when everyone was at church. My room's a den now but the closet wasn't touched."

I pulled out a thick, cream-colored sweater.

"My mother knit that. It's a fisherman's sweater. Not very stylish, but warm."

I looked at the half-shirt that hung off her shoulders. "Maybe you should keep it."

"Too baggy for me. And, anyway, I've changed my style. I like things super tight."

She reached in and pulled out a pair of sweatpants. "These are the coziest things ever. Feel the inside."

I did. It was fuzzy.

"There are leg warmers in here too. And hats and mitts. I picked all the heavy stuff because I know how cold you get."

I pulled on a hat with a big bobble on top. It had orange-and-yellow stripes around the top and bottom and sandwiched in the middle were multiple Snoopys skating round and round in a circle.

"I have a story," I said. "If you'd like to hear it."

She sat on the bed and patted the spot next to her. "I was just about to ask for one. You and me, we're on the same wavelength."

On the same wavelength. I liked that.

She put her arm around me and ran her fingers through my hair.

"I just need to think of one," I said.

"Take your time."

I thought about who she was and what she was all about.

"I've got one."

"I'm listening."

"So, there was this nun and she really needed to pee so she walked into a bar and—"

"Um, Bun? This sounds more like a joke than a story."

"What's the difference?"

"A joke ends with a punch line."

"Oh. It was in the Funny Stuff section of a magazine. I don't know if that means it has a punch line or not."

"Oh well. Just keep going."

"So it was really loud with music and stuff, and every now and then the lights would go out, and when they did everyone howled with laughter. But when they saw the nun, they all went silent. She asked the bartender if she could use the bathroom and he said, 'Yeah, okay, but just so you know, there's a statue of a man in there and the only thing he's wearing is a fig leaf,' and the nun said, 'That's okay, I'll just look the other way.' So the bartender showed her where the bathroom was and after a few minutes she came back out, and when she did everyone in the whole entire place gave her a round of applause. She asked the bartender why and he said, 'Well, now they know you're one of us. Would you like a drink?' And she said, 'I don't understand,' and he laughed and said, 'You see, every time someone lifts up the fig leaf, the lights go out. Now, how about that drink?'"

Big Eyes didn't say anything at first but then she burst out laughing. "Holy bleep! That is the funniest thing I've ever heard in my whole life! I'm gonna tell my bleepin' mother that joke. I'm gonna tell it right to her bleepin' face. She'll probably have a bleepin' heart attack and die, and then I'll have it engraved on her bleepin' tombstone, and then I'll never have to say, 'No, I didn't go to bleepin' church this week,' and she'll never be able to look at me like I am the devil again."

I didn't know what to do 'cause the rainbow on her eyelids was running down her face, so I went and got Chef who came in and held her for a whole load of Mississippis.

~

Halfway through the party Cher came home and I was glad
'cause I liked her as much as Chris. She said, "Get off that
beanbag chair and come sit with me," so I squeezed onto the
couch beside her. She held my hand and I rubbed my thumb
over her shiny red polish. She smelled sweet, like the pear
galette Chef had made the night before.

When Busker Boy and Chef took a break from singing I
said, "Let's play a game."

Everyone looked at me like I was a strange alien being,
but when I pointed at Pop Girl and said, "You first," Busker
Boy smiled.

I asked her, "If you could be an animal, which one would
you choose and why?"

She looked around as if the answer was floating in the
room. "I'm not sure."

"How about a polar bear?" I said. "Or a penguin. 'Cause
you're a bit cold, a bit icy."

Big Eyes moved her finger back and forth across her
throat, and I asked her if she was okay 'cause I knew there
was an international sign for choking but couldn't remember
what it was. I figured everything was fine though, 'cause Cher
was Chris and Chris probably knew the Heimlich maneuver
and would be doing it by now if Big Eyes was in danger.

Pop Girl said, "Are you going to let her talk to me like

THE AGONY OF BUN O'KEEFE

that?" and I wasn't sure who she was talking to, but then Busker Boy said, "She doesn't mean any harm," and Pop Girl said, "She's a bitch," and Busker Boy flinched, but I just said, "You could actually use that as an answer to my question if you want 'cause a bitch is a female dog."

Then things got weird 'cause Chef starting singing "The Bitch Is Back" with his eyes half closed, and Pop Girl said, "You are the rudest, most obnoxious little asshole I've ever met," and Cher zigzagged her finger in the air and said, "Don't you talk to her like that, you tarted-up little tramp."

Big Eyes told everyone to calm the bleep down but no one was listening. Somehow, though, Busker Boy's soft, quiet voice cut through the noise. "I think it's time you left." I stood up but Cher pulled me back down, and then Pop Girl looked at me and said, "Well happy friggin' birthday!" I opened my mouth to say it wasn't my birthday but Cher told me to shush.

The slam of the outside door shook the living room window.

"Maybe," said Big Eyes, "you should think about things before you say them."

"I was just trying to get to know her better."

"Well we've seen her true colors now," said Cher, "and we've got you to thank for that."

"Still," said Big Eyes. "The whole polar bear thing was a bit harsh."

"I can't help it if she doesn't like icebreaker games. *Reader's Digest* said they were sure to be a hit."

Everyone laughed but Busker Boy had a pang, I could tell. He said, "Go to bed now, Bun." So I did.

~

I didn't like falling asleep without him 'cause of "The Tell-Tale Heart," which was weird 'cause I'd fallen asleep alone most of my life.

I hung on to the last bit of wakefulness in my body—it was a tiny spark of light through my eyelids. Sometimes it would flicker, bright then dim, but something inside me kept it powered on until I heard Busker Boy slip into his bed on the floor. Then the spark burst and died.

FIVE

In the morning he said he wasn't mad and it was probably for the best.

"You didn't have to tell her to leave. I don't expect people to like me."

"It's not that she didn't like you. She was envious, that's all."

"Of what?"

"The fact that we're close."

"In that case, *jealous* is the appropriate word. Envy means you want something that someone else has, like a car, but jealousy is the fear of losing someone 'cause of someone else."

"Hmmmm. I never knew that." He passed me a catalog. "It was on the doorstep when I went for the papers."

On the cover a small girl and a smaller boy snuggled

together in an armchair, a stocking hung in the background. The words *Christmas Wish Book 1986* hung above them.

"Why would you give me this?"

"Thought you might like to see it."

"Why?"

"It'll be Christmas soon. If something catches your eye, we can see about getting it."

"Like what?" I turned to a random page. "An electric pencil sharpener? It's the 'quick and easy solution to dull-ended pencils!'"

"Are you . . . mad?"

"Oh, look. What everyone needs. A rock tumbler. 'Transform ordinary stones into gem-like treasures.' Pretty please, can I have one?"

"You *are* mad."

"Or how about this? 'A truly unique gift, this handsome reproduction of an old cigar-store Indian brings your home vintage charm.' Is that your wish this year?"

"Close the book, Bun."

"Look at his big feather headdress. Isn't he amazing? Three and a half feet tall and only $99.99. Why don't you get yourself one if you love this bleepin' catalog so much!"

"Close the book and pass it to me."

He wasn't expecting me to throw it. It hit him in the chest. "I don't want anything for Christmas!"

I flopped back on the bed and buried my head in the

pillow. I didn't normally cry, but I felt like I could. So I did.

He left the room and came back with a glass of water. "Sit up."

I took a drink.

"Are you missing home? Is that it?"

"No."

"Then what is it?"

I had no idea. So I said so.

"I don't know what your Christmases were like at home . . ."

A day like any other after my dad left.

"But we're going to have a nice time. I promise."

No one ever promised me anything before.

"Chef's cooking a feast. Turkey and all the trimmings."

Way in the back of my eyes I felt a stinging and it wasn't just the promise or the turkey or that he was the nicest person I'd ever met, it was the look on his face when the Wish Book hit him in the chest. I wasn't sure how to say it 'cause I'd never said it before and I could feel the words churning in my tummy and when they rose up they came out choked and croaky. "I'm sorry."

He caught a tear with his thumb. "It's okay to have a meltdown. You're only human."

It was more than the crying. I pressed rewind. It helped to explain. "The catalog. I threw it. I hurt you. I'm sorry."

I felt a pang. Being human was hard.

He looked me in the eyes. "Don't worry, Nishim. I forgive you."

"Nishim?"

"It's a term of endearment, in my language."

"Like how Chris says my ducky?"

He laughed. "Yes. Something like that."

"Braid my hair?"

He spun me around gently by the shoulders and combed my hair with his fingers. He gathered every strand and wisp loosely at my neck. I closed my eyes. After a few gentle twists and tugs a long braid hung between my shoulder blades.

~

We went busking to help pay for Chef's feast. Busker Boy was playing "Imagine" when a pickup pulled up and a guy in the passenger seat said, "Get a job, you drunk Indian!" I stepped toward the curb. "He doesn't drink."

"An Indian that doesn't drink?"

I pressed rewind. Pop Girl had said the same thing. *You don't drink? That's ironic.* There was a connection there that I didn't want to make.

"Nishim! Get away from there!"

"Is he bossing you around, sweetheart? They're like that when they're drunk."

Busker Boy grabbed my arm and yanked me back.

"Get your hands off her, you dirty Indian!"

Busker Boy pushed me away. "Run."

These were the rotten people he'd warned me about, I could tell, so I clung to the arm of his jean jacket with both my hands, so he wouldn't be alone, but these rotten people, they didn't care, they just tossed me aside. I fell back onto the sidewalk and watched as they punched and kicked and punched and kicked, and I said, "Stop! He gave me a shirt when I was cold."

I heard noises that I didn't like and they were coming from Busker Boy, but then they stopped and I hoped that meant he was thinking of something nice, like fresh strawberry jam. A lady in a violet coat helped me up and said, "Thank the Lord for good Samaritans." I pushed her away and ran back to the rotten people, but they got in their truck and drove away.

I rolled him over. He was bloodied and bruised and one side of his face was so scraped it looked like that beef in the tin, the one with the bull on the label. I felt sick.

He said, "You need to go." His voice sounded like a record on the wrong speed. I said no but he nodded at two cops heading toward us. "They'll take you back to your mother. Go. I'll meet you around the corner."

I leaned against the side of the Royal Bank with my eyes closed. My mouth was filled with strawberry jam and my head was filled with a song.

I don't know how long I was there.

"It's time to go."

He sounded like he was talking with his mouth full, and it turns out he was 'cause he stopped to spit out blood.

The splat on the ground hurt my heart.

The walk seemed longer, 'cause of his grunts and groans. I wished he knew the script from Jimmy Quinlan. Reciting it would help take the pain away.

I had lots of questions but asked just one.

"Why do people care if you are Innu or if you go to church or whether you're a Cher or a Chris?"

He didn't answer. He just took my hand. And that was enough.

~

Chris and Chef helped him up the stairs and sat him in a kitchen chair. Chris kept asking him pointless questions like "What day of the week is it?" and "Can you tell me today's date?" Busker Boy's mouth was sore so I answered all the questions for him. Chris got mad and told me to shut up.

Chef offered Busker Boy a skinny cigarette.

Chris said he should take it. "It'll dull the pain."

I wanted to be dulled too.

"Can I have one?"

Everyone said no.

Big Eyes said she was going to call the cops but I told her they already knew.

"So are they out looking for the bleepholes who did this?"

"Are you friggin' kidding me?" said Chris. "Of course they're not."

"But that's their job," she said. "To catch the bad guys."

He laughed a really horrible laugh. "Are you really that naive?"

Busker Boy held his forehead. "Please stop."

"I'm sorry, but her friggin' stupidity astounds me. Then again, I don't know why I'm so surprised. A pretty, straight, white girl like her would never understand."

"Don't take it out on her," said Chef. "It's not her fault the world's a messed-up place."

Chris left the room. I thought it was 'cause he was mad but he came back with a black bag. As he passed Big Eyes he put his hand on her shoulder, looked her in the eyes and said he was sorry. I wondered if he was going to say sorry to me for saying shut up but he didn't.

He took out a light and shone it in Busker Boy's eyes. "Come here and help me, Bun."

He asked me to get the stethoscope while he and Chef peeled off Busker Boy's shirt. He listened to Busker Boy's breathing and felt his ribs.

I looked for footprint shapes in the bruises.

"Go get the Tylenol, Bun. It's in the medicine cabinet. Extra-strength."

When I came back he was dabbing Busker Boy's cuts with something that made him flinch.

"You're hurting him."

"Has to be done, my ducky."

Dragon Man appeared in the doorway. "What's this? An orgy?"

Big Eyes pointed at Busker Boy. "Does this look like a bleepin' orgy?"

"It kind of does the way the faggot's straddling the Indian."

"What's a faggot?" I asked.

Chris walked toward the door. "Get lost. We pay our rent. We don't need to take shit from you."

"Speaking of rent," said Dragon Man, staring at Busker Boy, "you owe me money."

"He just gave you rent," I said. "The other day."

Dragon Man rolled his cigarette back and forth across his lips. "Come here, little one. It's time we got acquainted."

Chef stood as close to him as he possibly could. "I think it's time you left."

Dragon Man laughed and went upstairs.

~

That night as I got ready for bed I heard Busker Boy playing his guitar. His song was broken. The words came out without meaning. They were puffs of empty breath. They floated around like bits of dust. They were sung by a skeleton, a frame with nothing inside.

As I brushed my teeth I wondered, could a fourteen-year-old have a heart attack?

Chris woke Busker Boy every hour throughout the night to check for concussion.

They woke Arthur O'Malley every hour too. He was in the Old Brewery Mission with Jimmy Quinlan. When he spoke his bottom lip went up under his nose. I tried to copy it but it was hard 'cause I had top teeth. His eyes were big and he had a strong East Coast accent, which I liked doing. He liked it at the mission. He said they treated him like a gentleman. When he went to bed they checked on him every hour to make sure his heart was "still tickin'." He said, "I'm all right don't worry about me, don't worry. I'm all right." He put his hand on his heart when he said the "still tickin'" part, so I'd do the same whenever I'd recite it.

In the middle of the night I heard Busker Boy sobbing and I didn't know what to do, but then I realized Chris was lying with him and I heard him whisper, "Don't worry, you'll be all right," and I wanted to ask, "Will I be all right too?" but my mother always said, "It's not all about you, Bun O'Keefe," so I didn't.

~

Busker Boy wasn't at the end of my bed; he was still asleep on the floor, and seeing him there made me sad but I wasn't sure why. I went to the kitchen and Chef said, "Hey, little Sally Lunn bun, want some breakfast?" and I said I wasn't hungry. He gave me a slice of toast anyway and said, "Do you want to talk about yesterday?" and I said, "I should have given him the bed. He's all bashed up and he's on the floor, and even though he's asleep, I can tell he's tired, and I didn't even think to offer him the bleepin' bed."

"No one expected you to give up your bed."

"He asked me once if I was strong and I said yes but I couldn't hold onto his arm."

"You're a kid. You couldn't have stopped what happened yesterday."

"He said we were close, but you know what's bad about being close?"

"What?"

"The good times are great, but the bad times, they feel way worse."

Chef shrugged. "No one said life was easy."

I said, "Do you have fifty cents?"

"Yeah. Why?"

"I want to go get a paper."

84

He reached in his pocket and separated two quarters from his coins. "Want me to come?"

"No, I can do it."

I didn't plan on leaving the nicest person I'd ever met. But when I got to the store my legs wouldn't stop walking. I took it as a sign. Maybe it was time to move on. To a mission, where no one would care about me and I wouldn't care about them. Or, even better, I could move back with my mother, where there was no caring at all. Maybe life would be simpler that way.

The cold air made me lose my breath but I kept on walking anyway. I cut through the park to get to Water Street. I was halfway through when I saw Chris sitting on a bench under a tree. He was dressed up in a smart wool coat. It was navy blue and had six big buttons. Peeking out from under the collar was a blue and yellow striped scarf. He looked real nice and seeing him there gave me that rumbly kitten feeling. I loved that feeling and knew I'd never feel it again if I went back to my mother. Not unless I got myself another kitten. Which I wouldn't. That house was no place for an animal.

I turned around and went back to the store. Then, with the paper tucked under my arm, I walked back to my temporary accommodations.

~

For the next few days, Busker Boy was sore and stiff. All he wanted was to be left alone but Chris said he needed to get up and about. Chef brought him breakfast but said if he wanted lunch or supper he'd have to come get it. Busker Boy shuffled to the table like an old man. I put my hand on his elbow, like a boy scout helping an old lady cross the road. I brought him Tylenol whenever he needed it, and my legs always stopped at the store, and I read the headlines to him 'cause he wasn't talking very much, so I figured the muscles that moved his mouth were too tired.

When he was uncomfortable he made noises that made me feel the pain too. I suggested he recite a script. "Repeat after me," I said. "Jimmy Quinlan, aged thirty-eight, has been drunk for twelve years." He didn't see the point but I said, "It really helps. Not that I've been in a lot of pain, but when I was alone in my house I'd get weird thoughts, like Who am I? or Am I real? and it was kind of painful 'cause a sore stomach always came with it. But becoming a narrator always made it go away." Busker Boy looked more pained than ever. "I can't do this, Bun. Not now."

Chef and Big Eyes were worried. They said Busker Boy wasn't himself. Chris said, "Give him time."

He wouldn't take my (his) bed no matter how many times I offered.

He slept a lot. When he woke he stared at the ceiling.

One morning, after I got the paper, I went to the bench

I'd seen Chris sitting on. A big tree above me creaked and moaned. I said, "You okay, tree?" Its biggest branch gave a nod. I said, "What about my friend? Will he be okay too?" The wind picked up and all the smaller branches whispered, "Yes, yes, yes."

Back at home, I said, "I bought the paper and talked to a tree." He barely noticed I was there. I knelt next to his bed on the floor and said, "Want me to braid your hair?" and he said he was sorry, which was a weird answer, so I asked again and he said yes. I combed his hair with my fingers and I twisted and tugged until a long braid hung between his shoulder blades. I asked him if it looked okay and he said yes. I didn't believe him but figured lying was okay if you meant no harm.

The next morning he came with me to get the paper and I held his elbow. I figured if I was a boy scout I might get a badge.

It took ages, but soon he wanted to busk again. He said he couldn't afford not to. He didn't walk like an old man any-more and his face looked less pained, but at night, when he took off his shirt, I was sure I could see footprints.

~

We sat around the kitchen table getting ready for Christmas. Big Eyes and Busker Boy were stringing popcorn, Chef was baking molasses cookies, and Chris was teaching me how to make paper snowflakes.

"This must be your mother's favorite time of year," said Chris.

I must've looked confused 'cause he added, "She liked to shop, right?"

The answer was yes, but not in the way that he thought, and I wished he'd never asked 'cause she didn't belong with us there in the kitchen where things were Christmassy and nice.

"I don't want to talk about her."

"I'm sorry," said Chris. "I didn't mean to upset you."

"I'm not upset. I just don't want to talk about my mother 'cause it'll only remind me how stupid and annoying I am."

"You are not stupid or annoying," said Busker Boy.

"Well I was to her," I said. "And that's a fact. The day I left she said, 'Where's that expresso machine I bought today?' I said, 'I think you mean espresso,' and I was going to tell her that *espresso* literally means 'pressed out' 'cause it was an interesting fact, but she told me to get out. She said, 'I'm sick of your sauciness, always talking back, why can't you hold your tongue for once? Go on! Get out!' So I did."

"I always wondered why you left home," said Big Eyes. "I figured it was something big but this . . . this is kind of small but big at the same time, you know what I mean?"

I didn't. Things were either big or small. They couldn't be both.

"I never meant to be rude," I said. "I just had a voice that never got used. So I tried to make conversations whenever I could."

I unfolded a paper snowflake. "Did you know that all snowflakes have six sides?"

Busker Boy left the room.

I was going to press rewind but Chris said, "He'll be okay, love. He just needs a few minutes."

"What about your dad?" asked Big Eyes. "Was he nice?"

"He had a nice voice. He used to sing about a man making potions in a traveling show. He called me Bunny. He left 'cause of the shopping."

Most things about my dad were a blur, except for his red hair and beard. I remember thinking he looked like Yukon Cornelius, from the Rudolph Christmas special, only less cartoonish. He took me to Dairy Queen, once. The day I got my glasses. I had a chocolate dip. He told me I looked smart.

Chef placed a plate in front of me. On it were two warm cookies, fresh from the oven. "Guess how much iron is in one tablespoon of blackstrap molasses?"

"I don't know."

"Three point five milligrams."

"Hmmm."

I ate my cookies then took over Busker Boy's popcorn job until Chris said I should go to bed.

Busker Boy was already in his comforter.

I took off my Frankie sweatshirt and looked around for my (his) flannel shirt. He pointed at my undershirt. "Was that okay? To get Wonder Woman?"

"Yeah. That was okay."

"Not too young?"

I looked at his battered face and felt a pang. "I have a story," I said. "If you'd like to hear it."

He didn't smile but his eyes went crinkly. He patted his comforter.

I sat down cross-legged and started. "So when I was little there were Underoos commercials on at Christmas time. There was one where a little boy holds up a package of Spiderman Underoos and says, 'My favorite heroes are Spiderman and my Uncle Fred,' and then a little girl holds up the Wonder Woman ones and says, 'My favorite heroes are Wonder Woman and my mama,' and I wondered what made her mama a hero? Did she save someone from a burning building or something? It was one of the commercials I liked to repeat and I tried to say 'and my mama' just like she did, but I was never sure if I was doing it right 'cause the girl was sweet and cute and I wasn't. At the end of the commercial it said, 'Be a Christmas morning hero, give Underoos.' There was no Christmas morning at my house, but when you gave me the Underoos, it reminded me of

THE AGONY OF BUN O'KEEFE

a time when everything on TV was snowmen and reindeer and mistletoe and even though I wasn't part of it, I kind of was, and it made me feel that Christmas spirit people talk about. It was a nice change from regular days, you know? 'Cause it was different."

It was supposed to make him feel better, my story, but for some reason he looked worse. It was too much to rewind so I just let it drop.

He pointed to the closet door. "It's inside."

"What is?"

"The shirt."

I'd forgotten I was looking for it.

I slipped it on and changed from my jeans into the soft, gray sweatpants that Big Eyes had given me. When I climbed into bed, something was hanging over me. Not literally. It was a feeling. Like when I'd start a book at home then lose it in the piles of junk. Something felt missing. It was 'cause he'd walked out earlier. And I didn't know why.

"I'm sorry I walked out earlier."

It was like he could read my mind.

"I just don't like the thought of you being so alone, with no one to talk to, that's all."

"There are worse things. Like being Anne Frank."

"And I am really, really sorry for saying you were frustrating. And that it was no wonder your mother kicked you out. You are not annoying. You are lovely. Never change, Nishim. Not for anyone."

And just like that the lost book feeling was gone. The missing pieces were filling in and I felt as whole as I'd ever been in my whole life, so I said good night, closed my eyes and waited for the spark to burst.

SIX

The next day was Christmas Eve. On the way home from busking we picked up Big Eyes from her shift at the candy store. Busker Boy said I could get something so I filled a bag with mini candy canes. Pop Girl was behind the counter.

Pop! "How may I help you?"

Busker Boy passed her the bag, which she dropped roughly onto the scales.

After he paid he said, "Merry Christmas."

Pop! "Piss off."

The three of us walked back to the house. Big Eyes said it would be her first Christmas away from home. Busker Boy said, "You can always go back," and she said, "To rosary beads and nightly prayers? No thanks."

Chef and Cher were in the kitchen. Christmas music blared from the ghetto blaster and our paper snowflakes hung from the ceiling. Cher put her arms around Busker Boy and danced him into the room singing "Last Christmas." Busker Boy played along, twirling and dipping Cher like a ballroom dancer. Big Eyes told him he had the patience of Job. Cher said, "Who's Job?" and I said, "You know, from the Land of Uz," and Cher said, "I've seen that movie a thousand times and trust me there's no Job," and I said, "Not Oz, Uz, from the Bible." Cher said, "You read the Bible?" and I said, "I tried but I like non-fiction better."

We played charades in the kitchen so Chef could guess while he cooked. I did the Grinch by swaying back and forth singing, "Fah who for-aze! Dah who dor-aze!" and Cher said, "What the hell, Bun?" but Big Eyes shouted, "Cindy-Lou Who," and when I said, "Close," she guessed right.

Sometimes, at home, I'd turn on the TV and radio at the same time, making sure that one was playing music and the other was talking. Real parties were much better.

The table was set with a red-and-green tartan cloth and there were wine glasses at every place, even mine. Chef served tourtière. "A French-Canadian tradition," he said. "I made mine with moose."

Cher said the crust was to die for. I said it was really good but I wouldn't kill myself over it.

Cher lifted her drink. "Compliments to the Chef."

I clinked my Purity syrup against their wine.

I can't say for sure, but if I was to take a guess, I'd say we all had the rumbly kitten feeling.

Dragon Man came home. On his head was a Santa hat. "Come sit on my lap and tell Old Saint Nick what you want for Christmas."

Busker Boy stood up so fast his chair fell over. Cher tugged his arm. "It's not worth it."

Chef brought Dragon Man a piece of pie. "Christmas is a time for kindness."

Big Eyes said, "He doesn't know the meaning of the word." Dragon Man mumbled thanks and went upstairs.

~

When it got late, Busker Boy said I should go to bed or Santa wouldn't come.

"Go on," he said. "Go get ready for bed. It's almost midnight."

Big Eyes burst out crying.

"What in God's name is wrong?" asked Cher.

She could barely get the words out. "It's . . ." She pointed at her wrist. "It's . . ."

Cher examined her hand. "Are you in pain? Did you sprain it?"

"She's not hurt," I said. "She's pointing at a watch that's not there. 'Cause she's thinking about midnight mass."

Chef took a puff of his skinny cigarette. "Holy crap. How the hell did you figure that?"

"Me and her, we're on the same wavelength."

Busker Boy stood up. "We'll be late, but Catholic masses go on forever, right?"

Big Eyes smeared the rainbow across her eyes. "Are you serious?"

Cher pulled on her thigh-high boots. "To the basilica!"

~

We skipped down Water Street singing Christmas songs, even Cher in her high heels, even me, a girl who'd never skipped a day in her life.

Chef suggested "Do They Know It's Christmas," and Cher said, "Dibs on the Boy George part!" After Busker Boy sang the Paul Young bit, Cher came in with the line about spreading a smile of joy, and it was so perfect everyone doubled over laughing, and Big Eyes said, "Oh my bleepin' bleep we'll never get there at this rate."

We sang the "feed the world" part together.

Singing, I discovered, was a great way to use your voice.

The basilica was big and grand, like something out of an Italian architecture book. Cher put her arm around Busker Boy and said, "If I'm struck down by lightning, will you revive me?" People turned to look as we slid into the last pew. I sat next to an old woman who was wearing a plastic rain bonnet. She nodded toward Chef and said, "What in the name of God is that on his head?" and I said, "Hair," and she tutted and said, "I never saw the likes of that in my life." People tutted at Cher too, but she smiled as if they'd given her a compliment. The priest at the front droned on and on and I must have drifted off 'cause the old woman next to me elbowed me. She reached in her pocket and pulled out a hard candy. I looked at Busker Boy. He nodded so I took it. He mouthed "thank you," and I mouthed back "why" 'cause I hadn't done anything, and he shook his head no and pointed at the old lady. It looked like she was praying, so I practiced in my head for next time: thanks, thank you, thanks a lot, wow, thanks.

When everyone formed a line in the center aisle I got up to join them but Chef said, "Stay where you are, little Sally Lunn." Cher walked it like a runway, one hand on her hip, the other flicking her hair off her shoulder.

A lady came to our pew and talked in angry whispers. Big Eyes covered her ears and ran out. Chef went after her and then Busker Boy told me to get Cher. She was disappointed when I said it was time to go. "This place is a friggin' riot."

Big Eyes stood outside under a big arch, crying into Chef's chest.

Cher put her arms around them and so did me and Busker Boy.

On the walk home someone yelled pansy out a car window. Cher did her runway walk again. "You show them, sister," said Chef.

The fast walking made me lose my breath so Busker Boy gave me a piggyback. I put my cheek next to his, and he said, "Don't forget to hang your stocking when we get home," and I said, "I don't have one," and he said, "Yes you do."

It was red felt with a snowman on it and my hands shook when I held it.

"Don't go getting all emotional now," he said.

All emotional. Me.

He told me to hang it on the fireplace in the living room. So I did.

~

Santa stopped coming when my dad left. I figured it was 'cause my mother turned me invisible.

Even Santa wasn't magic enough to see ghosts.

I still believed in him though.

In *Miracle on 34th Street,* Kris Kringle said, "Just because every child can't get his wish that doesn't mean there isn't a Santa Claus."

I liked that. It made my empty stocking a little less disappointing.

Eventually, I gave up on Christmas.

But when Busker Boy gave me the red felt stocking, I thought, Maybe I'll start believing in Santa again—he'd definitely find me now.

Busker Boy turned me visible.

~

It felt like something was different when I woke but I wasn't sure what. By the time I got downstairs I was sure.

They said, "Merry Christmas, Bun!" and I said, "It's here," and Chef sang "Christmas Time Is Here" from Charlie Brown, and they all joined in, and I said, "No. I mean, IT came."

Chef passed me an orange juice. "Santa's not an 'it.'"

"Not Santa. My period."

They came at me all at once. My juice went flying. "We did it! Oh my God! We did it!" There were high fives and hoots and hollers and Big Eyes said, "It's a bleepin' Christmas miracle," except she didn't say bleepin', and Chris sang "I'm Every Woman," and Busker Boy thanked Chef for all his good cooking and I said, "I can get pregnant now," and Chris said, "Jesus Christ, Bun, I hope that's a fact not a goal," and I said, "I have no goals."

~

In my stocking there was a box of Turtles, a small Funshine Care Bear, my own Love's Baby Soft, a slap bracelet, a neon pink wallet, a candy cane and, in the toe, a clementine.

"Thank you," I said. "Thanks a lot. Wow, thanks."

"We all chipped in," said Big Eyes.

Busker Boy handed me an envelope. "This was Chef's idea."

It was sealed with a rainbow sticker. I brought it to my nose. Chef laughed. Inside was a small plastic card. It said A.C. Hunter Library.

"Who's Cherilyn Sarkisian?" I asked.

"We couldn't use your real name," said Big Eyes. "In case they come looking for you."

"No one's looking for me."

"That's Cher's birth name," said Chris. "Beautiful, isn't it?"

I said it out loud, "Cherilyn Sarkisian."

If I hadn't used my voice in a while, it'd be a name I'd definitely repeat.

"You can borrow books for twenty-one days," said Chef. "And there's no limit."

I slipped the card into my new wallet. "I'm going to borrow a book for each of you," I said. "That'll be my Christmas gift to you."

I asked if I could say grace before we ate. They looked at me funny but said yes anyway. I recited Reverend Bill

McCarthy's words to the men at the Old Brewery Mission.
"Bow your heads and silently utter a prayer of thanks-
giving and thanks to God for his blessings. Good luck, have
a good meal and enjoy yourself. No seconds, okay?"

We ate turkey and potatoes and carrots and turnips. The
savory dressing was the best and I washed it all down with
Purity syrup. I tried to share my Turtles for dessert but they
wouldn't take one. "They're all yours, my ducky."

The coffee table was covered in bottles. Everyone
drank from them, except me and Busker Boy. We had egg-
nog instead.

We sat on the floor around the coffee table and played
Trivial Pursuit. We ate Pot of Gold and Terry's Chocolate
Orange. For the first time, I knew it was Christmas not just
by the carols and snowmen and sales that I saw on TV.

Chef leaned back and shared a skinny cigarette with Big
Eyes. I sat on the couch behind him and played with his
Mohawk. I brushed my hand along the top of it. It was like
a broom.

"Christmas is bleepin' awesome," said Big Eyes. "I feel
like Santa's elves sprinkled me with happy dust."

Then she giggled for longer than people normally
giggled.

"She inhaled, didn't she?" said Chris.

Chef laughed. "First the f-bomb, now this. Finally, she's
free."

Busker Boy strummed his guitar and Chris said, "Hello, you the new butler?" and Busker Boy laughed and said, "Well, it's been a long time since I've been the new any- thing!" and I knew they were doing the Bing Crosby and David Bowie bit from Bing Crosby's *Merrie Olde Christmas* 'cause we had the VHS tape at home. It was one of my favorites. Chris said, "Sir Percy lets me use his piano when he's not around. He's not around, is he?" and I said, "It's Percival. Sir Percival." They did the whole bit, and when they sang "Peace on Earth/Little Drummer Boy," I had a bad feeling in the pit of my stomach 'cause it reminded me of sitting alone in a dark house with an empty stomach thinking I was having a holly jolly Christmas by watching TV specials but I could see now it was all pretend. I wondered if it was too late to start a career in acting. Learning the scripts would be a breeze.

Dragon Man came downstairs and told Busker Boy it was time to pay up. Big Eyes said, "Merry bleepin' Christmas to you too."

I said, "Why don't you ask anyone else for rent?"

Busker Boy said, "Don't talk to him, Bun."

When Busker Boy left the room, Dragon Man winked at me and said, "I have a job for you, if you want it."

Chef told me to ignore him.

Busker Boy came back with an envelope. Dragon Man took it and said, "I miss my little Pocahontas."

Busker Boy lunged at him but Chef and Chris pulled him away.

I passed Busker Boy his guitar. "How about some Paul McCartney?"

Dragon Man smirked and walked away.

"You know the one," I said. "The mood is right . . ."

Pretending was good. I hoped he'd play along.

"Give me a minute, Nishim."

"You okay?" asked Chris.

He nodded and strummed his guitar. He didn't sing Paul, he sang John instead. The sad sounding one about war. A bad choice for pretending, I thought. Singing about simply having a wonderful Christmas time would have been better.

~

Before bed, there was a knock at the door. Chef went to answer it and came back with a small box. He passed it to Chris. "It's for you, Mr. Christopher Andrews."

"Who's it from?"

"Dunno. There was nobody there."

"Maybe it's a fan," I said, "from your shows."

His face lit up. "I like the way you think, my ducky."

When he opened the box, the light in his face went out.

He pulled out a card. *From Dad.*

Busker Boy moved next to him.

"What is it?" I asked.

He pulled out a smaller box. "Come here, Bun."

He said it was an inhaler, for my cough. When he was teaching me how to use it, Busker Boy squeezed his shoulder and I wasn't sure why, but then I saw that Chris's eyes were all wet. No matter how many times I pressed rewind I couldn't figure out what was so sad about an asthma inhaler.

~

I woke up to say read me something but Busker Boy wasn't at the end of my bed. I stared at the crack in the wall and hoped wherever he was he'd be back soon.

When he came back he had a bowl of oatmeal. "For you. From Chef."

Once, in a box from the thrift shop, there was a sign: Enjoy the Little Things. I never really got it. What little things? But then I saw the careful swirl of jam on top of my oatmeal. It was definitely a little thing and I was definitely enjoying it.

I let the steam fog my glasses. "Where's your paper?"

He pointed at the window. "Snowstorm. I'll get it when it clears."

"Oh."

"I can read some poems from my book if you want."

"Not if it's full of hithers and dithers."

I didn't like flowery poetry. The second last line of "A Dream Pang" hurt my head. "But 'tis not true that thus I dwelt aloof."

"Poetry isn't always doths and thous, you know."

"I know. It can be sneedles and thneeds."

He laughed. "Dr. Seuss?"

"Yup. My kind of poetry."

"You might like this too. It's kind of funny. How about I read one? See what you think?"

I wasn't convinced but said okay.

He settled in at the end of the bed and held up the book. *Poems for All the Annettes* by Al Purdy.

"This one's called 'At the Quinte Hotel':

I am drinking
I am drinking yellow flowers
in underground sunlight
and you can see that I am a sensitive man
and I notice that the bartender is a sensitive man
so I tell him the beer he draws
is half fart and half horse piss"

Busker Boy paused and raised his eyebrows. I grinned.

He read on about a bar fight and it was funny and real and raw. I renamed it "At the Old Brewery Mission" and imagined Jimmy Quinlan as the drunk friend that got slugged "ass-over-electric-kettle."

"Well?" he said when he was done reading. "What did you think?"

"I think I'd like to borrow that book."

He tossed it up my end of the bed.

I pointed to the window. "Is it clear yet?"

He looked out. "We won't be busking today. Not in this blizzard."

"Want me to tell you a story?" I asked.

"How about I tell you one?"

"You know stories?"

"Lots of them."

He pulled his comforter off the floor and wrapped himself up in it. "This one's called 'Wolverine Invited the Birds to the Drum Dance.'"

"Terrible title. Too long."

He tutted. "Quite the little critic, aren't you?"

Critic. Smartarse. Rude obnoxious asshole.

My face must've looked weird 'cause he said, "I'm only teasing."

"It's a fine title," I said. "Straight and to the point."

"Let's see if you think it's a fine story as well."

He began.

"One day, Wolverine, Kuekuatsheu, invited the ducks and a loon to a drum dance. When they showed up at the tent he suggested they close their eyes while they danced. After a while the loon opened one of his eyes and saw there weren't as many ducks as there were before. He looked at Wolverine and saw him picking up the ducks and twisting their necks one by one. The loon shouted to the rest of the ducks, 'Wolverine tricked us!' They all ran away, but as the loon was escaping Wolverine grabbed his tail feathers and pulled them off. And that's why the loon has no tail feathers."

I tried biting my lip but it didn't work. "New title. 'Ducks Are Stupid.'"

He laughed. "That's a bit harsh. Maybe 'Ducks Are Gullible' would be better."

"Who told you that story?"

"An Elder."

"Do you miss your community?"

"Yes."

"Why did you leave?"

"It's complicated."

"Will you go back?"

"Some day."

"What did those policemen say to you the other day?"

He paused. "The world can be an unfair place sometimes."

"I know. I read Anne Frank, remember."

"They called me a savage, Nishim. They asked me how much I had to drink and told me to stay out of trouble."

I read a book about Che Guevara once. He said that anyone who trembled with indignation at injustice was a comrade of his. What Busker Boy said made me tremble a lot. I said, "We should start a revolution," and Busker Boy laughed and said, "Who are you, Che Guevara?" I said, "No, but I'm his friend."

We listened to a snowplow go down the street and up the other side. We listened to it plow the next road over, then the one after that. The noise it made got fainter and fainter, and when we couldn't hear it at all I said, "Who's Little Pocahontas?"

Busker Boy looked toward the window. "Another day. Not now."

There was a collection of snow on the pane. It looked like lace. I said, "If it's stormy tomorrow, will you tell me another story?"

"I'll tell you one right now."

We spent the morning together, him talking, me listening, icy pellets pinging the bedroom window. Outside it was winter, but inside it was summer, and his steady, quiet voice floated through the room like a warm breeze, and his words swirled like dandelion seeds, and when they landed on me it was with a light touch. He told more stories about Wolverine, but I wasn't scared 'cause he said that if I ever met him, I'd be clever enough to outsmart him.

Chef knocked on our door at lunchtime. "Get up, you

good-for-nothing layabouts. I've made a pot of split-pea soup."

Busker Boy threw me my jeans. "I hope he made dumplings to go with it."

I had to suck in to fasten my button. "Look," I said, "they're almost too small."

The sight of it made his eyes water.

SEVEN

We busked a lot over the holidays. Every day he sang "Brown Eyed Girl" but changed brown to blue.

Once, in a box from the thrift shop, there was a sprinkler. I hooked it up and thought, Piece of junk, it doesn't work, but then I saw a kink in the hose. After I untwisted it, streams of water danced in the wind.

I think I might've had a kink, deep inside me, and I think it got untwisted when Busker Boy changed brown to blue. 'Cause suddenly all the blood in my body was able to rush through my veins at top speed. Busker Boy was right. It *was* possible to be more alive.

~

Chef took me to the library on New Year's Eve. I borrowed five books.

Night by Elie Wiesel

Cher: A Biography by J. Randy Taraborrelli

The Complete Galloping Gourmet Cookbook by Graham Kerr

The Lost Art of Profanity by Burges Johnson

Van Morrison: The Mystic's Music by Howard A. Dewitt

When the lady checked in the biography she said, "Oooh, I love Cher." I handed her my library card and said, "Do you know what Cher's real name is?" but before I could tell her, Chef cut me off and said, "Bun O'Keefe," and the lady said, "Really? That sounds like a Newfoundland name to me."

Afterward, Chef said he was taking me to the Newfoundland Hotel for supper, just the two of us. The head chef came to our table and asked me how I liked my duck à l'orange. I said it had great depth of flavor 'cause saying it felt like a rumbly kitten would be weird. He told me that Chef was a culinary talent and wouldn't be a dishwasher for long. Then he told Chef to get a real haircut, and I was going to say that, if anything, a Mohawk was more of a real hairstyle than most, but Chef just laughed so I did too.

When the dessert menu came Chef looked in his wallet and said, "What the hell. You only live once." He ordered us crème brûlée and as we ate it he said, "What do you think?"

and I said, "It tastes like a feeling but I don't know which one." He suggested melancholy, which surprised me and I said no, the complete opposite.

He asked me if I wanted to go to the top of Signal Hill. It was a long walk but I said yes 'cause my inhaler was in his pocket. Not that I'd need it. A couple of puffs in the morning and my breath was like the wind: easy, strong and free.

The whole city was lit up below us.

"Look," I said. "The basilica. See the crosses?"

He lit up a skinny cigarette. "Let's go to the ocean side."

We sat on the wall and looked into the blackness. I couldn't see the ocean but I could smell it. In the distance, a ship's light. Chef said, "What's it all about, Sally Lunn?" I said I didn't know.

"Do you really not have any goals?" he asked.

"Not that I can think of."

"I thought everyone had goals, even if it was just to get through the day."

"That's not a goal," I said. "It's an inevitability. Unless you're hit by a car or something."

He laughed. "Let's head home."

We took a cab as far as the park. Chef told me to stay close as we walked through the darkness but I wandered away from the path.

"Where you going, little Sally Lunn Bun?"

"I have a question."

He followed me to a park bench. I pointed at a small brass plaque screwed to the back. "Who's Jasper Hobbs?"

"How'd you know this was here?"

"I saw Chris sitting here once. It seemed like a nice spot so I came here one day, after I picked up the paper. The branches creak real loud but it's not spooky, it's more like a conversation."

"A conversation?"

"Yeah. Like after I'd say something, the tree would respond."

"You talked to the tree?"

"I had a Magic 8 Ball once and it always seemed to land on 'Don't count on it.' The tree is much nicer." I patted the bench. "Try it."

He sat down. "What do I do?"

"Ask it a question."

He looked up. "Will I become one of Canada's top chefs?"

I linked my arm through his. "Now we wait."

A few minutes later, a gust of wind and a long creak.

"Well?" he asked. "What did it say?"

"It said, 'It is decidedly so.'"

He shook his head. "You're cracked, do you know that?"

"Who's Jasper Hobbs?"

"He was Chris's boyfriend."

"Boyfriend?"

Chef laughed. "Good God, Bun. Don't tell me you didn't know Chris was gay."

"I never really thought about it."

"You know what being gay means though, right?"

"Yeah, I know. Once, on an episode of *The Love Boat*, Doc met up with an old fraternity brother named Buzz and Buzz introduced his boyfriend, Jim, as his cousin 'cause he was scared of Doc's reaction. But when Doc learned the truth, he said he was happy that Buzz had found himself and was happy. If Chris ever tells me he's gay, I'm going to say the same thing."

"I'm sure Chris thinks you already know. I mean, it's kind of obvious."

"It is? Let's see if the tree thinks so."

I looked up to the shadowy branches and said the words clear and slow. "Is . . . Chris . . . gay?"

The creak was short and loud.

"Wow," I said. "Signs point to yes."

"Well, duh," said Chef.

I rested my head on the bench. A single star twinkled in the distance. I read something once, about wishing on stars. I didn't see the point.

"How did Jasper die?" I asked.

"That is Chris's story to tell, not mine."

"How come Chris never talks about him?"

"Some memories are painful to remember. Even good ones. It's easier to push them to the back of your mind."

"Do you have memories in the back of your mind?"

He pulled me to standing. "Don't we all?"

Everyone was waiting for us at home. The coffee table was covered in snacks and we played games and sang songs and I didn't need to turn on the TV and radio to make a party 'cause we had party hats on our heads and cardboard horns in our mouths and at the stroke of midnight everyone cheered. Cher grabbed Busker Boy—"Come here, handsome"—and kissed him on the lips. Busker Boy kissed her back and laughed. "I'll never play for the other side you know," and Cher said, "Don't crush a girl's dreams, not on New Year's Eve." Busker Boy sang "Auld Lang Syne," which I knew was written by Robert Burns, who was Scottish, so I told everyone. Before bed I thanked Chef for the library and the Newfoundland Hotel, and he said, "You know what makes the Sally Lunn bun the tastiest bun of them all?" and I said, "What?" and he said, "It's sweet, light and delicate," then he sang, "Buy my nice Sally Lunn, The very best of Bunn, I think her the sweetest of any." Then he kissed my forehead and said, "Happy New Year, Bun O'Keefe."

~

The next day he was dead. Busker Boy found him in his room. The hotel had called to say he'd missed his shift. Chris had asked me to go wake him but Busker Boy said, "I'll go." Much later he said, over and over, "Thank God I went, thank God it was me that found him."

The three of them sat in a row on the couch. People came and went, police, ambulance, men in suits. And the three of them just sat. In a row. On the couch.

Chef was dead.

I wondered if he'd ever borrowed my dream, smelled a rainbow.

Maybe he did. Maybe the scent wasn't strong enough. Maybe he slid down the side and into a pile of mud.

I passed Busker Boy his guitar. He sang about someone who went to sleep hoping to never wake up. I hated it but when it was over I said, "Sing it again."

I felt more alive again. But in a bad way.

Chris said, "Come here, ducky."

I didn't normally cry.

But I was only human.

And being human was hard.

Dragon Man came home. "I got the call." He didn't look at me this time. He just said, "What a waste. Too bloody young." Then went upstairs.

It was the first day of 1987. And Chef was dead.

~

I asked why. No one had any answers.

There was no note, they said. No explanation.

But there was an envelope. Full of money. It was for Busker Boy.

"Pay the bastard off," it said.

I asked Busker Boy what that meant.

"It means we're getting out of here."

"When?"

"As soon as I find us a home."

I went to Chef's room. There was a bookcase next to his bed. I pulled out a French cookery book. Cassoulet, ratatouille, bouillabaisse. Real food that my mouth would remember. If he'd stayed around to make it for me.

I didn't blame him. He must have felt like Conrad in the book *Ordinary People*. Conrad said he was falling in a hole that was getting bigger and bigger. He ended up slitting his wrists. He didn't do a good job, though, 'cause he lived.

~

We stayed up most of the night. All of us together. So I was surprised when Busker Boy was up early the next morning with his paper.

"Want me to read you something?"

"Chef died."

"I know."

"And you bought a paper?"

"I buy a paper every day."

"You're acting like everything's normal and it's not."

"You need consistency. You need routine."

"You don't know what I bleepin' need!"

I'd never screamed before. It hurt my throat.

"Fair enough. You tell me. What do you need?"

"I need Chef back!"

He put down his paper and stood up.

"Maybe," he said, "what you need is space."

Alone in the room, I stared at the crack on the wall. It looked like a lightning bolt, fine cracks branching out from a thicker one, downward like an upside-down tree.

I wondered, for half a second, how it would feel to be hit by lightning. But I already knew. I was hit by lightning when Busker Boy came out from Chef's room. He'd had a pang. I could tell. And then, so did I. I'd never felt such pain.

I looked at the paper by my feet. He did know what I needed. I needed him to read me something.

But first, I clutched my pillow to my face and I sobbed. Then, I called for him.

"Read me something?"

He took my glasses off and passed me a tissue. I wiped

my eyes. He wiped my glasses. When he passed them back he said, "We'll need to get you a bigger pair soon."

He sat at the end of the bed. "Now. Let's see."

The snap of the paper, his eyes scanning the articles, his weight at the bottom of the bed, all of it part of the routine, *my* routine, the routine I never knew I needed.

"Here's a weird one. A three-hundred-pound woman died in a pile of garbage bags filled with junk. Huge house. A hoarder, apparently. The locals called the police when they hadn't seen her walking the streets with her wagon of junk. They're trying to locate her next of kin."

It registered in half a second.

"That was my mother."

He looked at me funny and said, "That's not a very nice joke."

"I don't tell jokes."

"What are you saying?"

"I'm saying, that's my mother."

"What?"

"The big fat hoarder. She's my mother. *Was* my mother."

He moved up to the head of the bed. "Are you serious?"

"I don't tell jokes and I don't tell lies, either."

"Are you okay?"

I felt perfectly fine. So I said so.

He held out the paper. "Want to read it?"

"No."

"I can take you back, if you want."

"No."

"Is there anyone you'd like to contact?"

"No."

"It says they're looking for her next of kin."

"I always thought that word was *king*," I said. "You know, like in 'We Wish You a Merry Christmas'?"

"Bun . . ."

"I expected it to rhyme. Good tidings we *bring* to you and your *king*."

"Bun. This is serious."

"Not really. I figured out it was kin eventually."

Later, I heard him tell Cher and Big Eyes. "I think she's in shock."

But I wasn't shocked. I wasn't anything.

With Chef, I was sad and all its synonyms—unhappy, mournful, heartbroken, sorrowful.

Now. Nothing.

It was the second day of 1987. And my mother was dead.

~

All day, they kept looking at me. Waiting for something. They said, "Want to talk about it?" and I said, "About what?" They said, "She was your mother," and I said, "Correct. She carried me in her womb for nine months."

I stood in front of the landing mirror. Did I look like her? Did it matter? Would I get fat? Was hoarding hereditary? Busker Boy appeared behind me. He brought a hand up and I flinched, and his eyes got real soft and he said, "Nishim. I would never hit you, you know that." One of the few things I knew for sure.

He combed my hair with his fingers. "Did she hit you?"

"No."

He gathered every strand and wisp loosely at my neck. I closed my eyes.

"We are all here for you."

"I know."

After a few gentle twists and tugs a long braid hung between my shoulder blades.

~

I started remembering more and more things. Memories I never knew I had. Pushed to the back of my mind, like Chef said. But why now? It wasn't any safer just 'cause she was gone.

I remembered too many boxes and bags in my bedroom. A complaint. A plea. An argument on the landing. Me with my facts about dust mites and molds and her with her *don't be a smartarse* reply. Me, armed with an old *Merck Manual*. *One speck of dust can contain 40,000 dust mites, which are major triggers of asthma.* Me, with a bottle of Vicks. *Take that for your cough and shut the hell up.* Me, crossing a line. *You're the reason he left.* Me, cowering under a raised hand, off-balance with fear, tumbling down the stairs. Thump. Thump. Thump.

It didn't hurt then and it didn't hurt now.

Nothing hurt now.

We went busking. It was one long off-key note.

When we got home Busker Boy said, "She hasn't said a word."

What did they want from me?

Chef's death was easy. You love someone, they die, you grieve. That's how it works on TV. But what if someone dies who you're supposed to love but don't? What then?

They told me I needed to be strong and I said, "You've got to be damn strong to be able to survive. These guys are not strong and they're not weak. They are in between and they're very fragile," and Busker Boy said, "Reciting from a documentary won't help, you know," and I thought, What the hell do you know? It's helped my whole life.

I walked past Big Eyes's room. She was on her knees. "Heavenly father, hear my prayer." I asked her what she was doing. She said, "Praying for you," and I said, "Why?" and she said, "Because you're hurting," and I said, "No I'm not. I'm nothing."

~

It was the third day of 1987. I said no to the newspaper. And busking too. What good was consistency? It never helped Jimmy Quinlan, not according to Reverend Bill McCarthy. He said Jimmy screws up his life for stupid reasons and goes round and round in circles, and forgets "the mission remains constant and has its hand extended for him in any condition that he might find himself—sick and poor or rich and sober. The mission remains constant."

Yet Jimmy Quinlan couldn't get off the booze. Reverend McCarthy said Jimmy was on a merry-go-round. At the time, I thought, Stop going in circles, Jimmy. Stop drinking and stay at the mission. But I get it now. Life was easier on a merry-go-round and I wanted on. I wanted to be spun out of my stupor.

I went to Big Eyes's room and plugged in her curling iron. When the light went red I gripped the rod. The pain they thought I should feel for my mother, I felt in my hand. Was that good enough? I was going to let go on five Mississippis but Big Eyes came in on three.

"Jesus Christ, Bun."

Chris put my hand in a bowl of cool water, then bandaged it with cream. He gave me a pill for pain I didn't feel.

I spent the rest of the day in bed, thinking about nothing.

Busker Boy came home late and said, "Why, Nishim?"

I had no idea. So I said so.

"Talk to me. I'm worried about you."

I owed him that much.

"I forgot how to feel when my dad left. But you reminded me how. Now, I've forgotten all over again."

"What can I do to make it okay?"

A brief flutter in my chest. "I don't know."

I pulled up the covers. Busker Boy sat on his comforter and strummed his guitar. He sang a song about bringing me a sense of wonder.

He'd done that.

But then he told me about the three-hundred-pound lady dead in the garbage bags.

And I was back in that house.

And the wonder was gone.

He told me to get some sleep and I said, "Turn off the light if you want," and he said, "No, I'll wait," and I said, "Turn it off," so he did.

EIGHT

Chris went to the funeral as Cher. Long black dress to match her long black hair.

Big Eyes wore rosary beads over a neon yellow dress.

Busker Boy wore a vest made from caribou hide.

Dragon Man laughed. "Nice duds, Tonto."

I wore my (his) flannel shirt and the soft gray sweatpants from Big Eyes.

Everyone around me had red-rimmed eyes. Tissues emerged from pockets and purses like a magician's endless scarf.

I didn't use a single one.

Not even when his hotel friends came back to the house and said nice things and smoked skinny cigarettes in his honor.

The head chef asked if I was okay.

I was fine.

Chris told him I'd lost my mother as well and it was too much to handle. He said, "She's shut down."

Shut down what?

Someone brought a fiddle.

They asked Busker Boy to sing. He tried. But his voice, which was usually a river, smooth and flowy, sounded like someone threw stones in it, jamming it up.

He put his guitar away and went to his room.

I didn't know Pop Girl was there until I saw her follow him.

Raised glasses. "To Chef!"

I went to the kitchen. I took a molasses cookie out of the tin and took a bite. It was like a mouthful of sand. I spit it out. I laid the cookie on the counter. It had one perfect bite missing, but nothing about it was perfect. It would never be whole again.

I cracked it into small pieces then broke the pieces into crumbs. I rubbed the crumbs between my fingers. Pulverizing them.

What's it all about, Bun?

He should have asked someone else. Someone with answers. Then, maybe he'd still be here.

Cher came up behind me. Pulled me away from the mess. "Oh, Bun. Just let it out."

"Let what out?"

A sigh. "Everyone's gone now. Why don't you turn in for the night?"

Busker Boy and Pop Girl were in my (his) bed.

"Doesn't she ever knock?"

"Give us a few minutes, Bun."

I closed the door and sat on the stairs to the attic. Dragon Man came home. He asked me to go upstairs.

So I did.

There were twelve steps to his door.

And five spindles on the back of the wooden chair.

He patted his lap three times.

"Come tell me a story."

I sat on his knees. He pulled me closer and slid his hand down the front of my sweatpants.

And I could feel again. It was a zing and a buzz. He nudged my head with his. When I turned he put his mouth on mine.

I could feel again but I couldn't. A numb jolt. A frozen shock. You *could* be two things at once.

I wanted to say stop but the muscles that moved my mouth wouldn't work. He moved his hand from Wonder Woman's blue and white-starred bottoms to her eagle crest top, and I thought, Why doesn't she stop him? She's Wonder Woman.

I counted Mississipis till a car horn beeped outside and he pushed me away.

"Make sure you tell Tonto we got acquainted."

I thought, Wait, don't you want to hear a story? and I knew I'd press rewind later 'cause it was a weird thing to think.

I walked downstairs on boneless legs. I looked at his (my?) door. Was it okay to go in?

I held the bannister all the way down the next flight and went to the nook. I wrapped his (my?) flannel shirt tight around me and curled into a ball on the beanbag.

I closed my eyes but the spark through my eyelids was back. It was hot and burning and I wanted it gone. Forever, maybe. Like Chef.

My mouth tasted smoky and stale so I imagined a spoonful of strawberry jam. It was fresh and sweet. It was a different time and a different place. It was Strawberry Fields Forever.

A hand on my thigh. I jumped.

"Here you are."

Was I there? Was I real?

"She's gone now. Come on, off to bed."

His arm around my shoulder. I wanted it there and I didn't want it there.

"You tired?"

I meant what I said
And I said what I meant . . .
An elephant's faithful
One hundred per cent!

"Yes. I'm tired."

Him on the floor, me in the bed. He reached for the light.

"No," I said.

"Okay," he said. "I'll wait."

I'd never made a promise before.

And then I did.

To the nicest person I'd ever met.

And then I went and wrecked it all.

Something was coming up my throat.

"I'm sorry, Nishim. I shouldn't have let that happen."

Let it happen? Did he know? He couldn't have.

"It's just, it's been a bad week and I just didn't care any-more, so when she followed me I let her. I should have told her to go, not you. This is your room, your bed. It wasn't right. I'm sorry."

I threw up.

"Jesus!"

He freaked out and called Chris, who cleaned me up and gave me a sip of water. "What a drama queen," he said. "It's just a bit of vomit."

"Will she be okay?"

"It's been a shit week. Two deaths? That's enough to make anyone barf up their guts."

I closed my eyes and when I opened them it was still night. Busker Boy snored softly. A sliver of light shone in from the crack under the door. I wondered, could Dragon

Man be a shape-shifter? Could he turn into a snake and slither under the door and into the bed?

Everything felt wrong. It was that lost book feeling multiplied by a million. And it was all my fault.

I crawled out of bed and climbed between the comforter folded in half on the floor. He lay on his side and I backed into him, close enough to feel the heat of his body but not enough to touch him. In the morning, I'd tell my first lie and say I fell out of bed in the night.

~

He believed me the first morning, but not the next.

"I don't think you should be crawling in with me. If you can't sleep, just wake me and I'll turn on the light. I'll stay awake till you fall back asleep, okay?"

The next night Dragon Man was standing over my bed. "Tell me a story."

I let out a scream that sent Busker Boy scrambling for the light.

He wiped sweat off my brow. "I will send for a dream catcher. My *ukumimau*, my grandmother, makes them. It will catch your bad dreams and let only the good ones pass through."

He was my constant.

But I was still spinning on the merry-go-round.

They whispered about me. "She's not dealing well. But at least she's not in shock anymore. At least she's grieving now."

My tears were for Chef and the broken promise, but I let them think they were for my mother too.

They said talking would help. Chef was right about memories. Even good ones could be painful to remember. I talked about them anyway. I talked about duck à l'orange and cooking for kings and queens and the view from Signal Hill at night.

I didn't talk about the broken promise.

'Cause he told me not to go up those stairs. And I didn't listen.

If I lost him, where would I go when I stopped spinning?

~

Busker Boy started calling me Shadow, 'cause I followed him everywhere. He didn't say it in a mean way. He said it with a smile. He announced his every move: "Come on, Shadow. Let's go get a snack." He even woke me up to get the paper.

Being his shadow was hard. I needed to be with him, 'cause of Dragon Man, but being with him reminded me of the bad thing I had done.

I wondered if you could get the DT's when you were fourteen. DT's were delirium tremens. Jimmy Quinlan got them when he stopped drinking. They caused shaking, night-mares and confusion, all the things I'd been feeling since I broke the promise. It made sense, in a way. 'Cause I was withdrawing too. Just like Jimmy. Not from alcohol, but from the world.

~

They sat around the living room singing Chef's favorite tunes and Big Eyes made Kraft Dinner and Chris said, "Chef would be rolling in his grave." I didn't like the sound of that. They apologized when I didn't eat. "Sorry, Bun, we can't cook like Chef." It wasn't the taste. I didn't deserve it, that was all.

They told stories about Chef and it felt good, like every-thing was normal. But then I slipped my hand under my shirt and felt the smooth, shiny eagle crest and got a funny feeling that must have showed on my face. "You okay, Bun?" I didn't like telling lies so I said I had to go to the bathroom, which was true, but I never got there 'cause Dragon Man was com-ing out and said, "Did you tell Tonto I damaged his goods?"

My mother bought damaged goods. Dented cans half off.

He stared at me, licking his lips, then smirked when the crotch of my light gray sweatpants darkened with pee.

Chris found me in my room and helped me look for my jeans.

"It's not uncommon, my ducky. Even at your age. Not after a traumatic event."

He left the room so I could change and I said, "Wait for me," so he stood outside until I was ready.

Back in the living room I sat as close to Busker Boy as I possibly could.

He sang a song that made our hearts hurt.

Big Eyes broke down. "He won't go to heaven. Not now."

"You don't really believe that, do you?" asked Chris.

"The Bible says 'Thou shalt not kill.'"

"So where do you think he is then?" said Chris. "If he's not in heaven?"

"In hell," she said, "according to my mother anyway."

Busker Boy cleared his throat. "Maybe we should talk about this another time."

"I don't give a rat's ass what your friggin' mother says," Chris said. "Chef's up in heaven sautéing artichokes and having a toke."

"Well I hope he's having fun," she said. "The selfish bastard."

Busker Boy stood up and nodded for me to do the same. "Come on. Time for bed."

"Selfish?" said Chris. "How can you say that? He was troubled. About what we'll never know."

Big Eyes wiped her eyes. "I just hope God forgives him."

Busker Boy paused at her side. "Maybe," he said, with a hand on her shoulder, "the one that needs to forgive him is you."

Later, in bed, I asked him what he'd meant.

"Once you forgive," he explained, "you can begin to heal."

"Does the person who needs forgiving heal too?"

"With forgiveness, everyone heals."

"Is Chef in hell?"

"No, Nishim. He is not."

"Where is he?"

"His body is in the ground. But his spirit lives on. He will return to this world in another physical form."

"What kind of form?"

He smiled. "Maybe he'll come back as a polar bear."

That night, I dreamt Chef came back as a kitten but Dragon Man turned into Wolverine and ate him. I screamed at the top of my lungs, but when I opened my eyes Busker Boy was sound asleep, so it must have been one of those silent screams. I wanted to fall off the bed and land on the floor next to him, but he told me not to do that anymore, he said to wake him, but that wouldn't be fair so I tried to drift off on my own by mouthing my narrator script.

For four nights and three days Quinlan has drunk no cheap wine, no hard liquor, no rubbing alcohol, no aftershave

*lotion. Last time he lasted nearly five months. This time
it's too early to tell. Every night now is a private agony,
every day a victory.*

Every night now is a private agony.

Every night now is a private agony.

I could feel Dragon Man's breath on my cheek and it
reminded me. Busker Boy told me not to go up those stairs.
And I didn't listen. I was the Queen of Sheba and deserved
everything I got.

~

He read from the entertainment section. "Aretha Franklin
was inducted into the Rock and Roll Hall of Fame. First
woman ever."

"I don't think I know her."

"Yes you do. You know, 'Respect'?"

A knock on the door made me jump.

"Never heard of it," I said. "Why don't you sing it for
me?"

He reached for the door handle.

Sing me the song. Don't answer the door. Sing me the
song instead.

A puff of smoke.

"Hello, little one."

I pulled up the covers.

"What do you want?" asked Busker Boy.

"Nothing. Just checking in."

"Good. Because we're even now."

Dragon Man winked at me. "Yes. We are."

"We'll be out of here as soon as I find us a new place."

"No rush."

Busker Boy shut the door in his face.

I didn't mean to say it out loud. But I did. And in my narrator voice, too. "For Jimmy and the thousands like him the mission is both a sanctuary and a threat."

"Why'd you say that?"

I moved down to the end of the bed, pretended to read the paper.

He put his arm round me.

"What's wrong, Nishim? You're shaking."

It was the DT's.

"Is it the landlord? Don't worry about him. He won't hurt you. Not while I'm around."

I was falling in a hole that was getting bigger and bigger.

"Come on, Shadow. Let's get some breakfast."

"I'll be down in a few minutes."

When he was gone I knelt on the floor. *Heavenly father, whoever, someone, anyone, please hear my prayers. Please, don't let him hate me.*

~

He was trying to swirl a spoonful of jam on top of a bowl of oatmeal.

"Sorry. I don't seem to have Chef's touch."

I stayed in the doorway. "I have something to say."

Chris and Big Eyes looked up from their breakfast.

Busker Boy leaned against the counter. "What is it?"

"I did something wrong."

"What did you do?" he asked.

I fiddled with the bandage on my hand.

"Just say it," said Big Eyes. "It can't be that bad."

I pressed rewind to the Wish Book. *Don't worry, Nishim. I forgive you.*

I looked up at the nicest face I'd ever seen in my whole entire life.

"I broke a promise."

I waited for it to sink in. It didn't take long.

His voice was tight. "Tell me."

Big Eyes looked at me, then at Busker Boy. "What's happening?"

My throat was dry. I wanted Purity syrup. I wanted to clink glasses and say Merry Christmas.

Chris caught my eye. "Bun?"

Busker Boy's chest rose up and down and he said, "Tell me," louder this time. So I did.

"I went up to the attic."

They all had a pang, I could tell.

His voice went from tight to barely there. "When?"

"After the funeral. You told me to give you a few minutes. So I went to the attic."

He put his face in his hands. "Jesus Christ."

I pressed rewind. *You told me to give you a few minutes.*

"I'm not blaming you. I should've waited outside."

He gripped the counter. "Tell me everything."

Twelve steps.

Five spindles.

Three pats.

Replaying it was re-living it.

"Can I have my oatmeal?"

"No," he said. "You need to start talking."

I slipped my hand under my shirt.

My favorite heroes are Wonder Woman and my mama.

That girl in the commercial, I was jealous of her. Or was I envious? I didn't know anymore.

"Bun," said Chris. "I know this is hard. But you have to tell us."

I stared at the floorboards. Had I really been worried about a beating heart underneath? Silly, stupid me.

Big Eyes sat me down. "Say something. Please."

I started at the end 'cause it was easier. "He pushed me away and said, 'Tell Tonto we got acquainted,' and I thought,

Wait, don't you want to hear a story? Wasn't that a weird thing to think?"

Suddenly it was winter inside and Busker Boy's words stormed around me like ice pellets and when they hit me it stung. "Start at the goddamned beginning and tell us what happened!"

"Can I have my oatmeal first?"

The bowl crashed against the wall. "What the hell happened up in that attic?"

Who was this person who threw things and whose voice went up and down and whose eyes looked scared and mad all at once?

Chris went to him, held his arms. "Calm down. This isn't helping."

Busker Boy dropped his head on Chris's shoulder. His voice cracked. "I just need to know."

My constant was broken and I needed him fixed.

"Nothing happened. I made it up. I'm sorry."

He left Chris and knelt by my side. "Nishim. You can do this. Please, be brave."

Maybe this time Jimmy Quinlan will find the courage to get off the merry-go-round.

"If I tell you, will you forgive me? 'Cause you said forgiveness heals and I need to heal. I really, really need to heal."

HEATHER SMITH

"Whatever happened was not your fault. I can promise you that. With all my heart."

No one ever promised me anything with all their heart before.

I decided to be brave.

"He patted his lap. And I sat on it."

"The landlord?"

"Yes."

"Then what?"

"He touched me under my Wonder Woman bottoms and my Wonder Woman top. He put his mouth on my mouth and . . ."

Busker Boy stood up and, with my head in his hands, pressed his lips against my forehead. Then, he bolted up the stairs.

Chris ran after him.

Big Eyes pulled me tight to her chest and said, "Oh, Bun," and I said, "I blamed Wonder Woman, but it was my fault; I should have stopped him," and Big Eyes's voice was really shaky and she said, "How could you, you're a child." We heard yelling then laughing then yelling then laughing then a smack and a slap and a "Calm down" and then a thump and a thump and a thump and a "Stop, you'll kill him."

Then, footsteps on the stairs.

"We need to pack, Nishim."

Chris looked at Big Eyes. "Us too."

Busker Boy put a hand on her shoulder. "You okay?"

She opened her mouth but nothing came out. Chris took her hand. "Come on. I'll help you pack."

Everything we owned went in Busker Boy's duffel bag. He whizzed around the room like a maniac while I stood in the corner, staring at the crack in the wall. I spoke in my best narrator voice.

"Four days out of seven start like this. They wait for a new day in one of the back alleys of Montreal. They spend most of their lives in back alleys. Jimmy Quinlan, aged thirty-eight, has been drunk for twelve years."

"Nishim. Please."

"There are about five thousand Jimmy Quinlans on the streets of Montreal, maybe even more in Toronto and Vancouver. No one dares guess the exact number of derelict human beings in Canada."

"Help me zip this up."

"The Old Brewery Mission—seven hundred beds for five thousand human beings."

He grabbed me by the shoulders. "Can you just shut up? We need to get out of here! What don't you understand?"

Everything was on fast-forward and I didn't like it so I pressed pause.

"Braid my hair? Please?"

His grip softened.

Chris and Big Eyes appeared in the doorway. "We're ready."

Busker Boy turned me around and combed my hair with his fingers.

Chris shifted from foot to foot. Big Eyes bit her nails. But Busker Boy took his time. He gathered every strand and wisp loosely at my neck. I closed my eyes. After a few gentle twists and tugs a long braid hung between my shoulder blades.

His voice was a river. "Are you ready now, Nishim?"

"Yes."

Outside, I could see my breath. I was going to explain about the moisture in our breath versus the moisture in the air but their foreheads were creased so I didn't.

Busker Boy said we should leave town and Chris agreed. Big Eyes said, "That's all well and good but where will we bleepin' go?"

"I know a place," I said. "But it's a bit messy."

NINE

Chris said there was a car in his father's garage with our name on it.

"No stealing," said Busker Boy. "Not on top of everything else."

"Who'd write our names on a car?" I asked.

"It won't be stealing," said Chris. "It's mine. I walked away from it. When I walked away from everything else."

He snuck into the big white house with the black trim and took the key. As we drove away from Winter Place, Busker Boy said, "If it's your car, what's with all the secrecy?"

"It's just easier this way."

I sat in the back with Big Eyes. She held my hand but stared out the window. Before we left St. John's, I asked if we could go up to Signal Hill. Busker Boy said, "No, we should get out of town," but Chris said, "Ten minutes, okay, Bun?"

We parked overlooking the ocean.

"He asked me what it was all about," I said. "I didn't know."

"Who does?" said Chris.

I asked Busker Boy to sing Chef's song, the one he said was the best ever. So he did.

And the rest of us, we sang the la-la-las and the na-na-nas.

~

Busker Boy and Chris talked up front in low voices, and I wished there was a narrator in the car providing commentary 'cause nothing they were saying was making much sense.

"You okay?" asked Chris.

"Not really. You?"

"Shook up. But he deserved everything he got."

"I didn't think he'd do what he did. I thought, if anything, he'd try to use her, like he used Shekau."

"He did it to get at you, the bastard. You should have split, after you got her out."

"I made a deal," said Busker Boy. "I had to stay."

"Well it's over now."

"Is it? Did you see what I did to him?"

"He'll be fine."

"He wasn't moving."

"He probably came around, after we left."

"I'm screwed either way."

"He wouldn't go to the police, not with his history."

When Busker Boy spoke next his voice shook. "I told her to leave the room . . ."

Chris took one hand off the wheel and squeezed his shoulder. "None of this is your fault."

"I should never have brought her home. She would've been better off on the streets."

"She would have been eaten alive out there, you know that."

"So instead I bring her home to that monster?"

"You did what you thought was best."

"I failed her."

"She'll be okay. We all will."

~

We turned off the highway onto gravel, a tree-lined road that I hoped would lead to my house.

"Jesus, Bun," said Chris, "you sure lived out in the boonies."

"Anyone else live on this road?" asked Busker Boy.

"There are a couple of summer homes, but that's it."

"So there's no one else living here right now?"

"Nope."

"Good."

A summer home family knocked on our door once. I was home alone and wasn't sure what to do so I just watched from behind a curtain. Two little girls in bathing suits stood waiting with their mom and dad, and just as they were leaving, my mother rounded the corner, dripping in sweat and pulling a load of garbage bags in her wagon. She spoke to the family, just for a minute, and when she came in I asked her what they'd wanted. She said, "They asked if any kids lived here. They got a big blow-up pool apparently." I waited for her to tell me more but she told me to unload the wagon. I'd never been in a big blow-up pool, so when the wagon was empty I said, "Did you tell those people a kid lived here?" She lay in her garbage bag nest with a twelve pack of doughnuts. "Nope."

We passed the laneways that led to the summer homes. "Now we keep going," I said. "For ages."

The car windows were closed but we could still hear the gravel popping and cracking under the wheels.

"There," I said. "Up on the left."

We turned up the drive and there it was—all gables and moldings and fancy trim.

I nudged Big Eyes awake. "Wow," she said. "I forgot you were rich."

The inside of my head felt jumbled. Why would she think I was rich?

I looked at Busker Boy. Didn't he tell them about the article? About the big fat hoarder?

I pressed rewind. I said she liked to shop, once. Was that enough?

We hid the car in the back and walked round to the front.

"Do you have a key?" asked Big Eyes.

A key? I barely left the house. "It'll be open."

I could feel myself changing as I walked to the door. With every step I grew a new layer of skin, each one thick and hard and tough.

I pressed rewind and walked in reverse. 'Cause how could I be Nishim through all those layers? Maybe with each step they would peel away, one by one, like an onion.

I walked backward into Busker Boy. He put his hands on my shoulders. "There's no rush. Let's sit in the car awhile." Casey Kasem's *American Top 40* was on. We listened from number ten ("Everybody Have Fun Tonight" by Wang Chung) to number four ("Walk Like an Egyptian" by The Bangles). If Big Eyes and Chris were wondering why we were all sitting back in the car again they never said. Big Eyes just curled up in the passenger seat and drifted off again while Chris sang along to the radio. Busker Boy sat in the back with me and waited.

I waited for Chris to finish doing the weird Egyptian arm-dancing thing and then said, "Okay. I'm ready."

When Busker Boy smiled the lines around his eyes went crinkly. Maybe, I thought, I don't need layers to be tough.

~

We stood squished in the front hallway.

"Ugh," said Big Eyes. "It smells like someone died in here."

She apologized right away. "Sorry, Bun."

"For what?" I said. "It's a fact. But the body would be gone by now. What you're smelling is a load of old junk."

We squeezed through the boxes and bags that lined the hall, and when we got to the living room, Chris said, "Jesus Christ, Bun. A *bit* messy?"

I think I grew up with fogged-up eyes because for the first time I could see the place for what it was. It looked like something out of a television news report. *This is Bun O'Keefe reporting live from the scene of a devastating tornado.*

"Why didn't you tell us?" asked Big Eyes.

"You never asked."

A mountain of junk filled the room. On the top of the heap were plastic garden chairs, stuffed toys, cases of canned goods, empty pop bottles and random pieces of sporting equipment. Underneath were half-crushed boxes of old books, musty magazines and broken toys, all of it thick with dust and spilling across the floor. I allowed my eyes to go to her corner for two Mississippis. Her mound of garbage bags was still there, overflowing with clothes and with a large indent in the middle. I used to pull her out of there when she'd get stuck. It was the only time we ever touched.

I wished I had my old eyes then, the ones I could barely see through.

Chris said the place was making his skin crawl. He picked up a can of potted meat. "No wonder you were malnourished when we met."

Big Eyes sneezed. "And had a nasty cough."

Chris flicked on a light switch. "Power's still on." He climbed over an old sewing machine table and reached for the thermostat. "It's friggin' freezing in here."

"You can turn it up," I said. "But it'll still be cold. I think it's 'cause of all the old junk on the vents."

He checked the phone on the wall. "Dead."

"It was never alive," I said. "We had no one to call."

Busker Boy started throwing things left and right, making a path from the living room to the kitchen.

He reminded me of Dig Dug, the video game character who dug underground tunnels. I only played it once 'cause the Atari she'd brought home had a broken fire button so I couldn't kill the meanies. The music drove me crazy and now it was back, all beepy and high-pitched and providing the soundtrack for Busker Boy's frantic tunneling.

"What the hell are you doing?" asked Chris.

Busker Boy plowed through the junk. "This place, it's not good for her asthma."

"I packed my inhaler," I said.

"Which you hardly need anymore. And we're going to keep it that way."

He threw open the back door and started chucking stuff outside.

"This will take weeks," said Chris.

Busker Boy lobbed a garden chair into the backyard. "Then it takes weeks."

~

We spent the afternoon looking through the piles of food for stuff that was in date.

Chris picked up a can of spaghetti hoops. "Chef would be appalled."

We had beans and crackers for lunch. Busker Boy barely paused to eat. He just kept dig-dugging his way through the house.

"I found flashlights," he said. "But someone needs to find batteries."

"Why do we need flashlights?" asked Chris. "We have power."

"We're supposed to be in hiding. The last thing we need is this house lit up like a beacon."

"We could make a secret annex with a secret door hidden by a bookshelf," I said. "That's how Anne Frank hid. If we made it windowless, we could use lights and everything."

Busker Boy's face got red. "We don't need a friggin' annex. We need goddamned batteries!"

He had sweat on his temples and his hands were shaking.

"Are you scared?" I asked. "You look scared."

Somewhere in the house something fell over. Busker Boy jumped. He looked at Chris. "I can't take this."

Chris reached out, placed his palm on Busker Boy's cheek. Busker Boy leaned into it and closed his eyes. He didn't look scared anymore.

I was thankful, then, for my unfogged eyes. Seemed I could see the good stuff as well as the bad.

~

There were three bedrooms in the back and two in the front. I said I'd take my old room, which was in the front. I even promised that I wouldn't use a light 'cause I'd be going straight to sleep anyway.

"Are you sure?" said Busker Boy.

For some reason I said yes.

Chris asked if there was a washing machine 'cause the blankets and sheets made his skin crawl. I told him it was somewhere in the basement under a pile of junk and when I suggested he wash everything in the bathroom sink with a bar of soap 'cause that's what I used to do, he said, "Jesus Christ, Bun, you poor thing." We decided to sleep in our clothes. Chris was so bundled he said he felt like the Michelin Man, but a dapper version 'cause he was wearing his fancy wool coat. I said, "Did you know the Michelin Man is also known as Bibendum?" and he threw his scarf around his neck and said, "I am Bibendum, Michelin Man's gay alter ego," and I said, "Don't you have a show at Priscilla's tonight?" and for a second he looked sad but said, "Whatever. It was a fun job but the pay was shit."

We helped each other clear the rooms of junk. Big Eyes wasn't talking so I asked her questions 'cause I wanted to hear her voice, but she answered everything with "Um-hm," even if it didn't make sense.

I wrapped my arms around her waist and said good night. "Um-hm."

Busker Boy told me to get ready for bed and when I was done he came in and said, "Are you sure about this?" and I said yes, but as soon as he left Dragon Man slithered under the crack, so I left my room and went to his and said, "Is it okay to change my mind?" and he said, "Of course it is." He left the room and a minute later he and Chris came in with my bed, first the frame, then the mattress. Our two beds were side by side just like at our temporary accommodations.

As I lay in bed I got the familiar feeling of the space around me getting bigger and bigger. I was a little kid again and I didn't like it. The room, the town, the country, the world, they all grew while I shrunk. I was a tiny speck in the universe, nothing.

"You doing okay over there?"

And just like that I was reminded. I wasn't a speck anymore.

"I miss the crack on the wall," I said, which wasn't really an answer to his question but it was what came to mind.

He left the flashlight on till I fell asleep.

~

What happened in the attic was on replay and it wouldn't stop no matter how many times I jammed on the button.

Dragon Man could slither anywhere.

I could just make out Busker Boy's shape in the dark.

I liked that he was in a bed and not on the floor.

A car horn beeped in my head.

Make sure you tell Tonto we got acquainted.

The whole thing was on loop. The stairs, the spindles, the chair.

I turned on my side to keep Busker Boy in sight.

~

There was no paper in the morning but he sat on the end of my bed anyway.

"Why didn't you tell them?" I asked. "About my mother?"

"That was your business."

I pressed rewind to the shock on their faces.

"This is a horrible house, isn't it? I'm glad I never realized it when I was living here."

"Every cloud."

"Every cloud, what?"

"Has a silver lining."

"What does that mean?"

"It's an expression—meaning you can always find something good in something bad."

"I don't get expressions. If you have something to say, you should say it."

"I see your point," he said. "Why beat around the bush when you can cut to the chase?"

He had a big grin on his face. I didn't know why.

"Does what happened in the attic have a silver lining?" I asked.

He flinched, like he'd stuck a knife in a toaster.

"Did I say something wrong?"

"No. You're just abrupt, that's all. There's never any warning."

"I'm sorry."

He smiled. "Don't worry. I should know by now to be prepared for anything where you're concerned."

"Like a boy scout," I said.

He laughed. "Yeah. Like a boy scout."

I stared at the ceiling. "I think about the attic a lot, do you?"

"I try not to."

"I think the answer is no," I said. "To the silver lining question. 'Cause as hard as I look I can't see one."

He was quiet so I guess he couldn't see one either.

"Who's Shekau?"

He got a pang. I could tell.

"Shekau's my sister."

"What's she like?"

"Beautiful inside and out. Just like you."

"Did she wear her hair in a braid?"

"Sometimes."

"Was the landlord mean to her too?"

"Another day, not now. Okay?"

"Can we read some Al Purdy?"

He pulled the book out of his duffel bag.

"Can I ask you a question?" he said. "Before I start reading?"

"Okay."

"Now that your mother is gone, will anyone be coming here to look for you?"

"My mom told the school I'd left with my dad. No one knew I existed. Even if they did, they'd have forgotten me by now."

"What about your father? If he finds out your mother has died, he might come back to get you."

"Don't worry; he's forgotten me by now too."

Busker Boy opened the book and thumbed through the pages. "How could anyone forget you, Bun O'Keefe?"

~

Big Eyes stood over a sink of soapy dishes.

"There's a pot of oatmeal on the stove. It'll be ready soon."

"Wow," said Busker Boy, "you've been busy."

"This house won't clean itself, you know."

For the first time in my life I could see the kitchen table.

"What time did you get up?" he asked.

She opened a package of paper towels and started wiping the bowls. "I don't know."

"You look tired," he said. "Why don't you take a break?"

She turned away from him. "I'm fine."

He laid a hand on her shoulder as she dished up the oatmeal.

She shrugged him off.

Busker Boy said, "Bun, why don't you tell Chris that breakfast is ready?"

As I walked up the stairs I got that lost book feeling. Big Eyes was grumpy and I didn't know why.

Chris wouldn't budge from his bed.

"Come have a cuddle," he said. "It's friggin' freezing."

"But we're having oatmeal."

"Five minutes, then we'll go down. Promise."

His wool coat felt itchy against my cheek.

"Do you like it here?" I asked.

"It's fine for now."

"What do you mean, *for now?*"

"Well we can't live here forever."

"Yes we can. It's called squatting. I saw it on a documentary about punks in England who took over an abandoned house. If we stay long enough, we'll get rights to this place. It's an actual law."

"And what will we live on? I don't think there are many drag queen positions out here in the middle of nowhere."

"Who needs a job when you live rent free?"

"And what about food?"

"The punks didn't care about any of that stuff."

He propped himself up on his elbow. "We're not punks. We're normal people."

I raised my eyebrows at him.

"Okay, maybe not normal. But we deserve a nice life just like anyone else."

"We can have a nice life here."

"No, Bun, we can't. I've lived a good part of my life in hiding and I don't plan on doing it again."

I played with one of the big buttons on his coat. "When did you live in hiding?" I asked.

"When I pretended to be straight to my family."

I didn't want Chris to have to live in hiding again, but what he didn't understand was that if we went back to St. John's *I'd* be living in hiding. Unless Dragon Man was dead, which I hoped he was.

I thought of Doc's fraternity brother on *The Love Boat*. "Did you ever pretend Jasper was your cousin?"

He looked surprised. "How do you know about Jasper?"

"I saw you on his bench once."

"You never said."

"Chef said it was your story to tell."

"You could have asked. It's no big secret or anything. It's just hard to talk about, you know?"

"Did he kill himself, like Chef?"

"No, my ducky, he had AIDS."

"I know about AIDS. It's been all over the news."

"Epidemics usually are."

"Did you have sex with him?"

"Jesus Christ, Bun. You and your questions."

"If you did, you could be HIV positive . . . are you?"

His mouth didn't move, but his face said yes.

"Don't worry. I'll still be your friend. I read this article, about the surgeon general. He says you can't get it through casual contact, but no one believes him. They think you can catch it, like a cold. There's this kid, named Ryan White, and he got AIDS and wasn't allowed to go to school. It's the whole strange alien being all over again. People are stupid. The surgeon general says we're fighting a disease, not people, and I agree. His name is C. Everett Koop. Isn't that a funny name?"

He didn't say anything again, and when I looked at him he was crying.

I caught a tear with my thumb, like Busker Boy did for me during the whole Wish Book thing. "I'm sorry. I'm too abrupt. I want to change but I don't know how."

He wrapped his arms around me.

"I wouldn't have you any other way, Bun O'Keefe."

TEN

After breakfast, Big Eyes gave us jobs to do. I was to sort the books, Chris was on clothes duty and Busker Boy was to get rid of any expired food.

"I'll do movies and music," she said. "If you're not sure about something just call out, *Keep or toss?* and we can help each other decide. We'll chuck all the *tosses* out in the backyard and at some point we'll take it to the dump."

"First things first," said Busker Boy.

He put batteries in an old ghetto blaster and popped in a tape. The Clash blared from the speakers.

"Jesus Christ," said Chris. "What the hell are they even saying? Wah-rah what?"

Busker Boy laughed. "White riot."

"They should learn to enunciate. And why are they always so angry?"

"They're not angry. They're passionate."

Chris pointed to the pile of tapes in front of Big Eyes. "See if you can find a Cher or a Babs so we can turn the angry punks off."

"Who's Babs?" I asked.

"Someone we won't be listening to," said Busker Boy. "Because if there's a Streisand tape in this house it's an automatic *toss*."

Chris wiped away an imaginary tear and sang, "You don't bring me flowers . . ."

Busker Boy rolled his eyes. "Here we go."

Chris walked slowly across the room, his eyes on Busker Boy, his song getting stronger and louder.

He grabbed the garbage bag of old food out of Busker Boy's hand and threw it aside.

Busker Boy laughed, and when Chris belted out the final, heartbreaking line, he laughed even harder. Chris ended his performance by collapsing into Busker Boy's arms.

"Can we just get back to work?" said Big Eyes. She picked up a VHS tape. "*ABBA: The Movie*. Keep or toss?"

"Keep," said Chris. "Duh."

"What about this one?"

Chris squinted at it. "*The Agony of Jimmy Quinlan*? Never heard of it."

The words in my book pile ran together, like someone had dumped a bucket of water over them.

Busker Boy sat up. "Can I see that?"

Big Eyes held it out. "Looks like a boring documentary about some old drunk in Montreal."

"Sounds like a load of shit," said Chris.

"It is," I said. "One of the worst movies I've ever seen."

I could feel Busker Boy's eyes on me as Big Eyes dropped the tape into the toss pile.

Poor Jimmy, he never had a chance.

~

Chris picked up a loaded laundry basket. "How about we go to the Laundromat, clean the bejesus out of this bedding?"

"No," said Busker Boy. "We need to lay low."

"We need a break," said Chris.

"They might be looking for us."

"Who's they?" asked Big Eyes.

"The landlord, the cops, your father."

Chris rolled his eyes. "My father's not looking for us."

"You took his car," said Busker Boy.

"*My* car."

Big Eyes sighed. "Can you guys stop bickering? It's all bad enough."

"I think we should stay put," said Busker Boy. "Until things settle down."

"We need bedding," said Chris. "We'll freeze to death without it."

"We'll be fine," said Busker Boy.

"Don't worry," said Chris. "We'll keep a low profile."

Busker Boy stood up, knocked the basket out of Chris's hands. "Screw the bedding!" he yelled. "I could be in deep shit here."

He sat down and put his head in his hands. It was dizzy on the merry-go-round.

"Look," said Chris, "I'm worried too. But I don't think he'll report you. He's got too much to lose."

"He hates my guts. He'd love to see me behind bars."

I imagined the nearest town swarming with cops, on the lookout for our unlikely foursome.

"He's the one who should be behind bars," said Big Eyes. "And if we had any sense, we'd report him."

"Don't be stupid," said Busker Boy. "Bun is a runaway with no family. She'll be put in foster care so quick your head would spin."

I wasn't good at thinking ahead 'cause there was barely ever anything to think ahead to. But Busker Boy, he had it all thought out. And I was glad. I didn't want to go into care. In *A Long Way Home* three abandoned siblings named Donald, David and Carolyn get put in homes and it doesn't work out that well, for any of them. It was a good movie, though. The guy who played Donald also played Conrad in *Ordinary People*. I wondered if he ever got any happier roles.

Big Eyes told Busker Boy not to call her stupid and he said, "Well, don't say stupid things," and I tuned them out until their voices sounded like the adults in Charlie Brown, all muffled and weird.

I sat by the laundry basket and brought a blanket to my nose.

"These don't smell too bad," I said. "I'd use them."

Chris knelt beside me. "Don't worry. I won't go to the Laundromat."

"Promise?"

He looked at Busker Boy.

"Promise."

~

Big Eyes went to her room during lunch. Busker Boy passed me a plate. "Why don't you bring this up to her?" I balanced it on my hand like a waiter in a cartoon. I knocked on the door three times and said, "Would Mademoiselle like some tuna on crackers?"

Her voice was hard and cold, an echo to my knocks. "Go away, Bun."

She didn't come out for an hour.

~

We worked all afternoon until Chris said he'd had enough. He collapsed into a patch of sunlight on the living room floor. "Let's have a siesta."

"Are you kidding?" said Big Eyes. "Look at all this work we have to do."

"Twenty minutes," said Chris. "We can have a communal nap, like a bunch of hippies."

Busker Boy laughed. "First of all, you are the least hippie-ish person I know. And secondly, *you* sleep on the floor?"

"Just goes to show how tired I am," said Chris. "It was so cold last night I barely slept."

"I'll have a siesta with you," I said.

Busker Boy nodded toward Big Eyes. "I don't think anyone will be having a nap as long as Sergeant Major's in charge." He took The Clash out of the ghetto blaster and put in an ABBA cassette. "Come on, Chris. If this doesn't get you going, nothing will."

Chris went back to his clothes pile, belting out "Mamma Mia" as he worked. When "Chiquitita" came on everyone sang, even Big Eyes who was still grumpy, and Busker Boy who didn't even like ABBA.

Just when it got to the chorus, Chris said, Holy frig! and ran out of the room with a small plastic bag. A few minutes later, it was Cher who returned, making an entrance like a beauty queen, all smiles and twirls in a snug-fitting dress. I jumped up and hugged her. "I've missed you!"

"It's a bloody Christian Dior," she said. "Can you believe it?"

She strutted back and forth, her long black hair swinging in time with her hips.

"Can you breathe in that thing?" I asked.

"Of course I can. It's like a second skin."

"It's a nice purple."

"Aubergine, darling, aubergine."

"It's probably from some dirty old thrift shop, you know," said Big Eyes. "Like all the other junk around here."

Cher adjusted the bust. "Guess what? I don't give a shit."

I said, "Isn't it making your skin crawl?"

"Skin doesn't crawl in Dior. It erupts in goose bumps."

Cher sat in Busker Boy's lap. "What do you think, handsome?"

"You look beautiful."

"Give it a feel, then, hot stuff. Pure silk."

Busker Boy laughed and stroked her thigh. "You don't give up, do you?"

"On you? Never."

The rest of us got back to work while Cher sat in a chair, legs crossed and chest out, her fingers running up and down the fabric.

I unearthed my old *Merck Manual* from the book pile and passed it to her. "Here. If you're not going to work you might as well read."

She held the book in both hands and stared at the cover.

"You never know," I said. "There might be something medical you don't know."

She said thanks, but I think she may have had that lost book feeling, and as she ran her fingers across the cover, I pressed rewind to see where I went wrong.

~

I went to Chris's room later that night. "I didn't give you the book 'cause I thought you didn't know enough medical stuff."

"I know."

"Do you wish you were a doctor?"

"Sometimes. Especially when my mom got cancer."

"I thought she died of disappointment."

"She did. I told her I was gay while she was in remission. She relapsed shortly after."

"My mother was disappointed in me too. She didn't care enough to die from it though. She ate herself to death instead." Chris opened his arms and I crawled into them.

I said, "You'd be a good doctor."

He smiled. "Too bad I'd have to be straight to become one."

"What do you mean?"

"Dad cut me off when he found out about Jasper. Said he'd start paying tuition again once I 'straightened up.' I had to drop out of school. Drag queen wages don't go very far."

"At least you had Jasper," I said.

Chris smiled. "Yeah."

"Too bad he had to go and die."

"Jesus, Bun."

"How did he get AIDS anyway?"

"He had a number of boyfriends up in Toronto, before I met him."

"Do you miss your canopy bed?"

He laughed. "Talking to you is like playing Ping-Pong."

"You play Ping-Pong?"

"Well, no. But the ball pings and pongs all over the place, right? Just like your conversations."

"You're going to leave soon, aren't you?"

"I can't live out here in the boonies. You know that."

"When will you go?"

"When things settle down."

"When will that be?"

"Soon, I hope."

I said, "Just so you know, there's nothing in the *Merck Manual* about dying of disappointment."

"I know. I'm sure the sadness didn't help though."

"Was she really that sad? About you being who you are?"

"Yes, my ducky. She really was."

I shook my head. "Too bad she never saw you in that aubergine dress. One look and she'd have totally understood."

~

The next morning Chris was gone. Big Eyes too. At first, we thought they were still sleeping until Busker Boy noticed the car was missing.

"He just had to go and clean that stupid bedding," said Busker Boy.

"What if they left 'cause they hate this stupid, stinky house?"

"They wouldn't do that."

"My father did."

"Come on, Shadow. Follow me."

We went to Big Eyes's room first.

"See? All her stuff is still here."

Chris's room was next. His fancy wool coat was on the foot of his bed.

My father wanted out so bad he took off and left his stuff behind. I wanted to believe Busker Boy, but I wondered if Chris and Big Eyes did the same.

We had a granola bar each for breakfast and went back to our piles. My book stack was getting smaller 'cause there were more tosses than keeps. I saved all the celebrity biographies for Chris. The cookbooks made me sad.

I wiped my hair out of my face. "Maybe they took a carload of bags to the dump."

"Chris would have waited for me for that."

"'Cause you're strong?"

"As an ox." He flexed his muscles, then said, "You look tired. Let's take a break."

We sat on the couch and looked around. It wasn't quite the Huxtable abode but we were making progress.

"My giant Wish Book of a home," I said.

"So that's why you freaked out."

"So much useless stuff."

I went to the window. "My dad left right before Christmas. He left all his stuff behind."

"They'll be back, Nishim."

"I hope so."

"Come here," he said. "Let's braid that hair before we get back to work."

I kept my ear out for the sound of gravel popping under the car wheels but it never came.

By lunchtime, Busker Boy's forehead was covered in wrinkles.

"They left, didn't they?" I said.

"No," he said. "They didn't."

"Then why do you look so worried?"

I moved over to his food pile. "Did you kill the landlord?"

"I don't think so. But I hurt him bad."

"He hurt me."

"I know."

I picked a tin of beans off the floor, ran my thumb across an indent near the rim. "Am I damaged goods? He said I was."

He took the tin out of my hand and said, "We're all damaged, in a way. But it's nothing that can't be fixed. You just have to kick out the dents from the inside."

~

It was almost two when we heard the popping sounds. We waited by the front door like TV parents waiting for their late teenagers. When Chris walked in with a basket full of neatly folded clothes, I was going to say, And what time do you call this? but Busker Boy lunged at him and pinned him to the wall. Laundry tumbled to the floor.

Chris said, "What's your problem?" and Busker Boy said, "You just had to go to the Laundromat, didn't you?" and I said, "Who wants to have a siesta?" and Busker Boy said, "I can't believe you'd put us at risk like that," and Chris said, "Let me explain," and Busker Boy said, "Explain what? That your pansy ass can only sleep on pristine bedding?" and my heart felt tight like someone was squeezing it, and then Big Eyes came in with a load of groceries and said, "What the hell? Let go of him right now!" so Busker Boy did, with a shove. Then he said something that sucked the breath right out of us. "Stupid faggot."

Hypoxia. That's what it's called when you're low on oxygen. Within minutes you can be brain damaged.

When everyone got their breath back Big Eyes said, "That was uncalled for," and Busker Boy said, "I am so sorry," and everyone's chests were going up and down, and I thought, Good, breathe in that oxygen, people. But then I looked in Chris's eyes and saw the biggest pang I'd ever seen, so I held my breath on purpose, hoping the lack of oxygen would go straight to my hippocampus and destroy my memory.

Chris pushed past us and ran upstairs.

"Chris called his father today," said Big Eyes. "We told him everything. He said he'd ask around, find out what's going on with the landlord. He was the one who did the laundry. And the groceries. We stayed in the car."

Busker Boy knelt down, stared at the bedding strewn across the floor. "I should have trusted him."

"Yeah," she said, as she walked out the door, "you should have."

I sat next to the laundry basket, brought a comforter to my nose. "This smells real good."

I put it in his face. "Smell."

"Bun—"

"Smell it."

"I'm not really in the mood—"

"Smell the damn blanket!"

Busker Boy looked up. "I'm sorry, Nishim."

I hugged the comforter to my chest. "It's not me you should be apologizing to."

"You know I didn't mean it."

I looked him right in the eyes. "I know that. With all my heart."

He gently tugged the comforter from my arms, brought it to his nose and smelled it. "This does smell good."

I nodded to the sunny spot on the living room floor. "You can fix this, you know."

He smiled. "It won't be that easy."

I gathered some sheets and blankets, pushed them into his hands. "Will you try? Please? I'll go get Chris."

I found him in his room.

I said, "You look like Rudolph."

He wiped his eyes. "My damn nose always gives it away."

I said, "He didn't mean it."

"I know."

"He's scared. If he gets put in jail, he'd miss us."

Chris's voice went soft. "I'd miss him too."

I held out my hand. "Will you come to the living room? He wants to make it up to you."

When we got downstairs they stared at each other till Busker Boy said, "I was angry and I wanted to hurt you," and Chris said, "Mission accomplished, look at the state of my face," and Busker Boy said, "There's no excuse for what I said," and Chris said, "It's not like I haven't heard it before," and Busker Boy said, "You should never have to hear those words, especially from people who love you," and Chris raised an eyebrow and said, "You love me?" and Busker Boy pointed to the floor. "Enough to make you a communal hippie siesta space."

When I was a kid and the snow was melting, I'd open the windows, and the breeze would come in all fresh and clean. That's what our siesta smelled like. Big Eyes said she had work to do, so it was just the three of us, and Chris said we were a hunk sandwich 'cause Busker Boy was in the middle, and I thought, Wow, Busker Boy was right, forgiveness really does heal. The sun beat in from the window and we basked in it. Chris said, "My dad was amazing today. I couldn't wait to get home and tell you," and Busker Boy said, "You're a good friend, Chris," and just as I was drifting off I heard Chris say, "You should be thankful my pansy ass likes clean bedding. These blankets smell friggin' amazing," and I thought, Like spring.

We slept soundly, toasty and warm, and when I woke I was happy 'cause Dragon Man never came. I figured he was like a vampire and I wondered if there was a way to lure him to my next siesta so that the daylight would destroy him.

~

Big Eyes called us into the kitchen.

"I found something while you were sleeping."

She laid some photos out on the table.

"They were in a shoebox, in the cupboard over the fridge."

In every picture a little girl posed on various pieces of furniture. The sofa and chairs were a mixture of upholstery and wood that stood grandly on legs that were curvy and carved. Each piece was set neatly around a large rug. Cabinets with glass doors lined the walls and on their shelves were vases and glasses and porcelain statues. It didn't look cluttered, though, and I bet if I dove in the picture I wouldn't see a speck of dust.

"Looks like a dollhouse," said Chris.

"Yeah," I said. "And that kid's the doll."

Chris laughed. "A sad, creepy one."

"I think *that kid* might be your mother," said Busker Boy.

My mother? In frills?

"She looks like a prop," said Big Eyes.

I stared at the unsmiling girl with the fixed eyes. "She looks like a ghost."

Chris fanned the photos out on the table. "This is fascinating. A young girl grows up in a pristine house, where everything is breakable, untouchable, held behind glass. Tormented by the sterile conditions she rebels, turning her house into a hoarder hell."

Busker Boy rolled his eyes.

"Do people burn themselves 'cause they were tormented by sterile conditions?" I asked.

They had wrinkles on their foreheads so I explained.

"She'd sit in the corner with a clothes iron plugged in next to her and she'd hold her hand against it to see how long she could last. It was like a game. I thought it was weird. I mean, why would you hurt yourself like that?"

They looked at each other and then Big Eyes said, "But, Bun, you did that exact same thing. With my curling iron."

"Yeah, that was weird, wasn't it? I don't know why I did that."

They were quiet for a minute and then Chris said, "Did she ever hurt you?"

"No. But she'd pretend to. Like, once I told her that the daily caloric intake of an average woman should be two thousand calories 'cause I'd read it in a magazine article called 'What Every Woman Should Know,' and she raised her hand like she was going to smack me. But it was good in a way 'cause otherwise how would I know I'd said anything wrong?"

Busker Boy stood up.

"Don't go," I said. "It's no big deal. Mostly she ignored me."

He paused, then kept on walking.

~

I stared at her garbage bag nest till I saw her.

I said, "Why do you hate me?"

Chris appeared behind me. "Who you talking to, Bun?"

"My mother."

He put his hands on my shoulders.

"Is that where she'd sit?"

"Yes."

He took my hand and brought me closer. We knelt near the indent.

"I sat here once. When she was out. I ate one of her doughnuts and shouted, 'Bring me a Pepsi, retard.' I didn't know she'd come home until she was halfway across the room. She said, 'Get out of my sight,' and when I didn't move fast enough she yanked me up and gave me a shove. I fell on a sink and bruised my ribs."

Chris got a pang, I could tell.

"Don't worry. I was a ghost. Ghosts don't feel much."

"Bun . . ."

"Yeah?"

"I think you're in denial."

"About what?"

"You weren't a ghost. You were a human being, with feelings. You've been traumatized."

"No, I haven't."

"Children are supposed to be loved, nurtured . . ."

"Mr. Rogers told me I was special every day."

"You can't get love from a television character."

"He sang a song, about how much he liked me, every part of me."

"Bun, it's not the same."

I pulled my hand away. "Why are you trying to make me feel bad?"

"I'm trying to help you. You need to come to terms with what's happened."

"Nothing's happened."

"Then why are you talking to a ghost?"

She was still there, giving me that look. It was the same look the rotten bad people gave Busker Boy that day.

I guess my mother was rotten bad too.

I reached out, poked a hole in a plastic bag with my finger. The material underneath was rough. Like denim. I scratched it with my nail.

"I looked up the word *retard* once. It means 'to slow down the development of something.' I figured she was making fun of me, 'cause I was small. But then, I saw an episode of *The Facts of Life* where Blair was tutoring a boy who wasn't very smart. They called him retarded and I thought, Am I retarded, too? My *Merck Manual* said people with mental retardation have sub-average intellectual functioning. I thought, If I have sub-average intellectual functioning would I be reading the

Merck Manual? Probably not. So I figured I wasn't retarded. My mother was just mean."

Chris took my hand away from the garbage bag. "Come here, Bun."

Chris had blue eyes and a tiny scar on the side of his nose. He told me once he got his eyes from his mother and the scar from falling off his bike when he was seven. I knew lots of things about Chris.

He pulled me to standing and we moved to the couch.

I said, "Were the garbage bags making your skin crawl?"

He laughed. "You know me well."

All I knew about my mother was that she liked powdered doughnuts and Elvis.

"I thought my dad left 'cause of the junk. But maybe he left 'cause of me. 'Cause I'm different. Maybe that's why she hated me."

Chris pulled me in close.

"Bun?"

"Yeah?"

His voice was a whisper as he sang.

"It's you I like . . ."

He sang it all, word for word.

Mr. Rogers was great.

But being nurtured by a real, live person was way better.

~

I thought I'd like to remember my mother as a hummingbird but in my dream she was a hippo with tiny wings that kept flying around my head, buzzing and buzzing and driving me mad. Dragon Man was back too, as a snake with a cigarette in its mouth that moved from the right to the left and back again. I woke up shivering and shook Busker Boy's shoulder, and I felt bad 'cause he was sound asleep, but I needed to tell him about the thought I'd been having, sometimes, not all the time, just at night in the dark, so I shook him, not roughly but gently, and hoped he would wake.

"What is it?"

"I want to talk about Wolverine."

He turned on the flashlight. "Back to bed. I'll come over."

I climbed back under the covers and made room for him to sit.

"Okay," he said. "I'm listening."

"I went to the drum dance 'cause I'm a stupid, gullible bird."

"You went to the drum dance because I let you down."

"You told me not to and I went anyway."

"What is done is done. There is no looking back, only forward."

"Sometimes I wish Wolverine had twisted my neck."

He was quiet. "It pains me to hear you say that."

"Sometimes I wonder what it'd be like, to be Chef living a happy life somewhere with no bad memories. I figure, if I wasn't here it wouldn't hurt."

"If you weren't here, *I* would hurt."

"I'd come back as a kitten and I'd live with you."

He smiled. "I don't want a kitten."

"They're not much trouble."

He looked at me in his thoughtful way. "Do you know what Nishim means?"

I shook my head.

"Little sister."

Not having layers was hard.

He caught a tear with his thumb. "Close your eyes now and get some sleep."

ELEVEN

I missed the crop-topped girl with the rainbow eyes, so when I found my mother's *People* magazine, the one with Princess Diana on the front, I carefully pulled out the Duran Duran article and gave it to her.

"Maybe you can hang it in your room," I said.

She barely looked up from her VHS pile.

"Thanks."

I said, "Are you mad at me?"

"No. Why would I be?"

"You haven't asked to do my hair or anything."

"It's not you, Bun."

"Then what is it?"

"If you tell her," said Busker Boy, "it might help."

"Tell me what?" I asked.

Big Eyes looked at Busker Boy. "I'm not sure."

"Go on," said Chris. "It'll be good for both of you. Go upstairs and have a chat."

As Big Eyes passed Chris he grabbed her hand and I thought, Wow, who needs words? 'cause they had a silent conversation of small smiles and encouraging nods, and it was beautiful even without knowing what it was all about.

She fluffed the pillows at the top of the bed and patted the spot next to her.

"Did the landlord hurt you too?" I asked.

"Not the landlord. Somebody else."

"Who?"

"My uncle."

"Did you tell him to bleep off?"

"I didn't know how to fake swear when I was five."

"You were five?"

"And six. And seven. And eight. He didn't stop until I was eleven."

I wondered if she ever wanted to be a spirit, like Chef.

"What made him stop?" I asked.

"I told. My mother called me a liar and told me to ask for God's forgiveness. But at least he kept his distance from then on."

"Every cloud."

"What?"

"Never mind."

"I'm sorry I've been out of sorts," she said. "It's just,

what happened with the landlord brought it all back, you know? My head's been all over the place."

"Claire Huxtable would've kicked your uncle's ass."

"Who?"

"You know, the mother from *The Cosby Show*. TV moms are way better than real moms."

She laughed. "Oh, Bun, I've missed you."

"I've missed you too."

She put her arm around me and pulled me in close.

"If I had any inkling about the landlord, I would've warned you. I thought the guy was a pimp, not a pedophile."

I pictured the word *pedophile* in my head. In Britain, it has an *a* in it. Between the *p* and the *e*. I wasn't sure that Big Eyes would find this fact interesting so I didn't share it. Plus, she was running her fingers through my hair and I didn't want to ruin the moment.

"I didn't know the landlord was a pimp," I said. "He doesn't look like the ones on TV. They wear fedoras and platform shoes. I'm not surprised though. He's a rotten person."

"He's a lot of things," she said. "The bleepin' bastard."

I smiled 'cause I hadn't heard *bleepin'* in ages, but then I covered my mouth 'cause smiling during a pimp and pedophile discussion seemed inappropriate.

"Did you think what happened with your uncle was your fault?" I asked.

"I did for a while. Especially with my mother bringing me to church all the time to repent my sins. I always wondered if what happened with my uncle was one of them. And when she wanted me to be a nun, I wondered if deep down she believed the stuff about my uncle and thought the convent was the best place for me. But as I got older, I was able to see that I had no control over what happened. And neither did you."

"I don't want to go back to St. John's. I'm scared to see the landlord."

"He'd be a fool to touch you again, after the beating he got."

"Did you ever see your uncle again?"

"He came into the candy shop last year. Bought a bag of malted milk balls. Waltzed up to the counter, as if nothing ever happened and said, How ya doin'?"

"What did you say?"

"Nothing. I let my fist do the talking."

"You punched him?"

"Not him. His candy. Smashed them to smithereens."

"Did he really *waltz* up to the counter?"

"Well, no. Not literally. I just meant he walked over without a care in the world."

"Oh. In that case you should have used the word *saunter*."

"I think you're missing the point of the story."

"No, I'm not. I even caught the symbolism."

"What symbolism?"

"You crushing your uncle's balls. If that's not symbolic, I don't know what is."

Big Eyes laughed. "You're a riot, Bun O'Keefe."

"Yeah," I said. "So I'm told."

~

Big Eyes joined us for a siesta. Halfway through there was a knock on the door.

Busker Boy sat up. "Nobody move."

"It's him," I said.

"Shh," said Chris.

"It's him. Make him go away."

"Quiet," said Busker Boy.

I stood up. Busker Boy grabbed my hand and pulled me back down. I brought his hand to my forehead and prayed like Big Eyes, but not about Heavenly Fathers. "The alcohol has almost completely worked its way out of his system. Quinlan's nerves are raw."

Chris growled at me. "Quiet, Bun."

Busker Boy leaned in close. "Just whisper it."

There was another knock, louder than the first, and it startled Big Eyes awake. Chris put his finger to his lips. My heart pounded.

"On a good day he could drink ten bottles of cheap Canadian sherry. Somehow today he's managing not to drink at all."

We heard the front door open.

I looked at Busker Boy. "I don't want to see him."

"Then close your eyes."

Chris whispered *shit*.

"If it's the cops, you guys know nothing," whispered Busker Boy. "If it's the landlord, take Bun upstairs."

The footsteps got closer, then a voice. "This is private property."

I felt Busker Boy's body relax.

"Sorry. We don't want any trouble. We'll move on."

"How did you know this place was empty?"

"We saw in the paper that the homeowner died."

"I only just found out," said the man. "I came as soon as I heard."

I opened my eyes but shut them again when I saw a man with a thick red-gray beard staring right at me.

"I'll have to put this place up for sale soon."

"Don't worry," said Busker Boy. "We'll be gone by tomorrow."

"Take your time," said the man.

Then he was gone.

~

At bedtime Busker Boy told me to close my eyes and hold out my hands.

"Now, open them."

The Agony of Jimmy Quinlan was in my upturned palms.

I said, "I didn't really want to throw it away."

"I know."

"I'm sorry I lied about it being terrible. Seeing it again made me feel funny, especially in front of all of you. I don't know why."

"Don't worry about it. You were embarrassed, that's all."

Is that what that feeling was?

I rubbed the cover with my hand. "This boring load of shit is like an old friend to me. Is that weird?"

"Not at all. We all have our quirks."

"Will you watch it with me sometime?"

"Sure." He tried the voice. "There are about ten thousand Jimmy Quinlans on the streets of Montreal."

"Five thousand," I said.

"Five, ten, what's the difference?"

"Five thousand," I said. I was surprised he had to ask.

"Chris is calling his dad tomorrow," he said. "If we're in the clear, what do you want to do?"

"I'm not ready to go back."

"Then we'll find somewhere to go wait until you're ready."

He laid the VHS tape on the bedside table and told me to get some sleep.

I tried, but I had something to say so I said, "Excuse me."

He laughed and put down his book.

"Yes?"

"I think I'm turning into a normal human being."

"What do you mean?"

"That was the first time I ever felt embarrassed."

He propped himself up on his elbow. "And that's a good thing?"

"Yeah. I mean, it didn't feel particularly good but it definitely made me feel more normal."

"You? Normal?"

I smiled. "Never going to happen, is it?"

His whole face smiled back at me. "I sure hope not, Bun O'Keefe."

~

The next day, while Chris and Big Eyes were in town, there was another knock on the door.

I hid in the kitchen.

Busker Boy came back with a note. "There was nobody there. Just this."

He read it aloud: "To the tenants, For the next six months all utilities will be covered by the homeowner. Should the tenants decide to stay beyond that time, a monthly rent will be paid directly to the homeowner. Please call the contact number below to negotiate a rate and set up a payment schedule."

I looked at Busker Boy. "Are we tenants?"

"I guess so."

"So we have a place to stay?"

"Looks that way."

"What about after the six months? What will we do then?"

He folded up the note and put it in his back pocket. "Why don't we take it one day at a time?"

He went to the fridge. "You can tell Chris's dad is a doctor. Look at this stuff—yogurt, apples, cucumber, carrots."

I said, "He bought hot chocolate too."

Busker Boy smiled. "Then you'd better put the kettle on."

I filled it with water and plugged it in.

Busker Boy passed me the powder. "That guy that was here yesterday. You know him?"

I turned away. "No."

We waited for the kettle to boil.

"What's that?" he asked.

"What's what?"

"The song you're humming. Sounds familiar."

"I wasn't humming."

He got his guitar and picked out the tune.

"It's 'Your Song,'" he said.

He loved me, my dad. He took me to school every day. He had a red beard and sang Elton John. He got me glasses when the world was fuzzy.

He hated me, my dad. He left and never came back. He left me in a big, stinky mess.

Busker Boy's voice suited "Your Song." It was perfect. *He* was perfect.

When he finished he said, "That's a real nice tune."

"Yeah."

I poured boiling water into two empty mugs. "Oh. I forgot to add the powder."

He put his guitar down and did it for me. "You okay?"

"I feel weird."

"In what way?"

"Like something bad might happen."

"Like what?"

"Like I might wake up some day and you'll be gone."

"That man was your father, wasn't he?"

"Yes."

"Sit down, Bun. I think it's time I told you about Shekau."

We stirred our hot chocolates and I leaned into mine, letting the steam fog my glasses, and Busker Boy opened his mouth to speak but didn't know where to start, so I helped him.

"Did she work for the landlord?"

He nodded. "She left our community without telling

anyone. It took me months to find her. She was selling herself down on Water Street. I grabbed her, said you're coming
with me. She told me to leave, said she was in too deep. But
there was no way I was leaving St. John's without her. So I
found out where she was living, broke the door down, told
the landlord she was coming with me—"

"Wait . . . she lived in our temporary accommodations?"

"Most of his girls lived in another house, but his 'Little
Pocahontas' was special. She told me he'd rescued her off the
street, promised her a job, a place to stay. I said, That's not
rescuing, that's recruiting."

"So did he let you take her? After you broke the door down?"

Busker Boy let out a laugh. "Not quite. He said I was
messing with the wrong person and to get the hell out. Shekau
stood behind him, said she was staying put. The next day I
was jumped. Black eye, broken ribs. But I never gave up.
I hammered the door every day. He said she was his best
girl. I said I'd pay him double what he made from her. I said
I'd rent her room, too, so he could keep an eye on me. I
wouldn't let up. I hung around for weeks. Eventually he gave
in. We set a price and I sent her home."

I didn't ask why he didn't just leave, once Shekau was
out. 'Cause Busker Boy was faithful, like Horton.

"There was nothing keeping me there but my word," he
said. "But I wouldn't have that bastard calling me a thieving
Indian."

It was like he could read my mind.

"Did the roommates know," I asked, "about Shekau?"

Busker Boy shook his head. "She'd told everyone she was a nurse's aide, up at St. Clare's Hospital. She made sure they knew how much she loved the night shift, because it was quieter than the day. It was a convincing story, crafted by the landlord himself. He said he'd kill her if anyone found out the truth. He had her scared to death. You should have seen her face when I told her I'd stay and she could go—she was so relieved."

Poor Shekau. Sounded to me like she was living in her own private agony.

"I bet she was glad," I said, "when it was all over and she was back home."

Busker Boy looked pained. "That's just it, Bun. She never made it back. I arranged the whole trip—the bus journey, the flight. But somewhere along the way she just disappeared."

"People don't just disappear," I said. "Unless they spontaneously combust. And even then there is usually evidence left behind, like a skull or a pile of ash."

I said sorry right away, before he could get a pang, or say, Jesus Christ, Bun, but he just looked at me and said, "Don't ever apologize to me for sharing the thoughts that you have in your head. They're honest and real and, more importantly, they're you."

I swallowed a lump that was lodged in my throat. "Don't worry. Shekau's out there somewhere. Maybe she just wanted to move somewhere else."

"No. She wanted to go home. I could see it in her eyes."

"But she has to be somewhere," I said.

I was getting that lost book feeling multiplied by a trillion.

"The police looked, Bun. She's gone. Shekau is gone. She's just another missing Indian girl."

I didn't like that word, *another*. I reached across the table and held his hand.

"It hurts me," he said. "Every single day it hurts me."

He looked into my eyes. "And that is why you will never, ever wake up and find me gone. I lost one sister, I won't lose another."

He didn't normally cry, but he made a gulpy noise and his shoulders went up and down, and he stood up and said, "Come here, Nishim." He pulled me close, wrapping me up tight in his arms, and it was the first time we'd actually hugged, which was weird 'cause I felt like I'd been hugged by him a million times, and I laid my head against his chest, and even though I felt bad that he was crying, I felt relieved 'cause I knew it meant he'd never walk out on me, not without telling me first anyway.

~

Chris and Big Eyes came back with good news.

"Guess what?" said Big Eyes.

"What?" said Busker Boy.

Big Eyes opened her mouth to answer but Chris blurted it out. "The landlord's been detained at the cop shop."

"What for?" asked Busker Boy.

"He recruited a twelve-year-old," said Chris. "Right out of the schoolyard."

"Jesus Christ."

"Within twenty-four hours her face was all over the media. There was a massive search, and when the cops found her, his operation was busted. He's in custody now till the trial."

Busker Boy stood up and looked around. "Where's my jacket?"

"Where are you going?" I asked.

"To experience the sweet smell of freedom. You coming?"

We walked down the back of the property and into the bush. Everything was dead and brown, but there were birds singing and the fresh air made me feel more alive.

We weaved our way through fallen trees until we came to a stream.

"I never knew this was here," I said.

"Listen," said Busker Boy.

It was a trickling—a musical, sing-songy trickling.

"What happens if we go back to St. John's and he gets out of jail and we see him somewhere?"

"Then we look the other way."

"Can we come here again?"

"Every day if you want."

"You know how you went looking for Shekau?"

"Yeah?"

"That was nice. No one came looking for me when I left."

"Your dad came looking when he heard about your mom."

"He just wanted to sell the house."

"You didn't see his face when he set eyes on you. He was looking for you, Nishim."

I pressed rewind. *I came as soon as I heard.*

"I think I'm gonna move back to my own room at the front of the house."

"Really? Okay."

Busker Boy pulled the note out of his back pocket. "The phone number that's on here, you want it?"

I looked the other way. "Nope."

We sat on a fallen tree, tossed pebbles into the stream.

"Bun?"

"Yeah?"

"We need to start thinking about your future."

"We do?"

"I want you to start studying, every day. So that when you're older you can get your diploma."

"Okay."

"You can be anything you want to be, you know."

"I can?"

"You're amazing, Bun O'Keefe. One of these days, you're going to knock the whole world dead."

~

Chris and Big Eyes were waiting for me when we got back. They said they were leaving the next morning. We had one last siesta, all four of us. We slept soundly, toasty and warm. And that night, Busker Boy and Chris moved my bed back to my room. As soon as I lay down I saw it—it looked like a lightning bolt, fine cracks branching out from a thicker one, downward like an upside-down tree. I got out of bed and went to the wall. I wanted to trace the crack but the ink was still wet.

~

I dreamt of fuzzy letters coming into focus and woke to the sound of my light clicking off.

"Go back to sleep," whispered Busker Boy, picking up Al Purdy off of the floor.

I must have fallen asleep reading.

A soft light glowed from the hallway. I raised my head to look.

"I had Chris pick up a night-light," he said. "Is that okay?"

"Yes. That's okay."

He slipped my glasses off my face and folded them. They were small in his hands.

I started to ask, "Would you be mad . . ."

But I didn't finish 'cause I wasn't sure.

"Mad about what?"

I pulled the sheet over my face. "That number in your pocket. If I asked for it."

He sat on my bed and tugged the sheet back down. "Of course not. Why would I be?"

"I don't know."

"Do you *want* me to be mad?"

"It would make my decision easier."

"What are you afraid of, Nishim?"

"That he'll want me back . . . that he won't want me back."

"What do you want?"

"I want to say hi. And then come back to you."

"Then that's what you'll do."

~

I didn't cry when Big Eyes and Chris left 'cause I knew they'd be back to visit.

Chris said he'd eat the face off me when he saw me next. Not literally, I assumed.

As they drove away Busker Boy said, "I don't know how we'll manage without a car."

I pictured him pulling my mother's old wagon around town.

"What are you smiling at?" he said.

"Nothing."

He passed me a slip of paper. "The phone line's been connected," he said. "I checked this morning."

He left the room when I picked up the receiver.

The ringing made my heart jump three . . . four . . . five times. The deep "hello" made it stop.

A funny thing happens when your heart stops—your voice doesn't work.

"Is that you, Bunny?"

When your heart stops, your legs stop working too.

"I think I died," I said, when Busker Boy found me.

He helped me up. "I think you fainted."

I passed him back the slip of paper. "Maybe I'll try again," I said. "When I'm older."

~

The sun was just coming up when we heard the knocking.

Busker Boy appeared at my door. "You know who that's going to be, right?"

I nodded.

"What do you want to happen?"

"I'm not sure."

He pulled a T-shirt over his head. "If you're not down in a bit, I'll send him on his way."

I hugged my knees to my chest and stared at the Magic Marker crack on my wall. This place was more of a home now than it ever was.

Even when the man with the red beard was in it.

He was never my constant. And never would be.

I pulled my flannel shirt over my Wonder Woman undershirt and slipped on my jeans.

Then, I went downstairs.

~

They were in the front hallway, talking. Even though my father was the bigger of the two it was Busker Boy who filled the space. His arms were folded and his muscles were bulging and his face looked serious. When he saw me he said, "Should we invite your father in?" and when I said yes, he nodded toward the living room. But my father didn't budge. Not until Busker Boy stared at him hard and said, "Relax."

We sat on opposite ends of the couch. Busker Boy stood in the doorway.

"Do you two want to be left alone?" he asked.

We answered no at the exact same time.

Then we said nothing. For a whole load of Mississippis.

"Your father wants to take you out," said Busker Boy.

And then I knew what he meant, about me being too abrupt. It didn't feel nice to be jolted by words.

"You don't have to," said the man with the red beard.

I looked at Busker Boy. "Can I?"

"It's okay with me."

"Should I?"

"That's up to you, Nishim."

I stood up. "Okay. I'll go."

My father stood up too, jingled his keys in his pocket. "Only if you're sure."

I hugged Busker Boy tight. "I'll be back," I whispered.

"I know," he said. Then he spoke to my dad in a voice that rumbled through his chest. "Two. Hours."

We drove away in a white convertible with shiny, red seats.

"Is this new?" I asked.

"Nope, 1974. I just take really good care of it. It's my pride and joy."

As soon as he said it, his face went funny. He opened his mouth but then closed it again.

When we hit the highway I wished I'd asked for a braid. I had to shout over the wind. "Where are we going?" I asked.

"To get you a new pair of glasses."

Another jolt. This time in my eyes. The wind would help hide the tears.

"Your friend, he said he'd wanted to take you for ages. Didn't have the money though."

I ran my hand along the smooth upholstery. "He takes good care of me," I said.

"Yes. I can see that."

We pulled off the highway. At a red light he pressed a button and the top went up. It got so quiet I could hear him swallow.

We drove up to a small building with an RX on the door.

"The optometrist's office is above the pharmacy," he said.

"*RX* comes from a Latin word meaning 'take,'" I said. "As in, take your medicine."

The way he looked at me, it was like I was speaking another language.

My seatbelt got stuck. His hand came close, to help.

"I can do it."

He pulled his hand back and said he was sorry.

Then he added, "For everything."

I pushed my thumb firmly on the button. When the buckle was freed I looked up and said, "Where were you?"

He looked away. "I went back to Nova Scotia."

"Back?"

"That's where your mother and I were from."

"I didn't know that."

"Newfoundland was supposed to be our fresh start. I thought country living would help, you know, with the shopping. But she still found a way to fill the house with junk. I couldn't take it," he said. "I had to get away. That place, I couldn't breathe."

"Maybe you have asthma," I said. "That's what I have. I figured it was environmental, you know, 'cause of the dirt and the mold and the dust, but maybe I got it from you 'cause asthma is hereditary too."

He turned back to face me with watery eyes.

"What did you do," I asked, "in Nova Scotia?"

"I started over. From scratch."

Erased, I thought. Like a drawing. And I was a tiny speck of rubber that he blew off the page.

"We could have started over together," I said.

He put his face in his hands and sobbed.

Above the glove compartment there was a brown panel, trimmed in silver, and on it there were raised silver letters. I traced them with my finger. *M-U-S-T-A-N-G*. I traced them over and over till he stopped crying.

He wiped his eyes with his sleeve and cleared his throat. "When I moved to Halifax," he said, "I remarried."

"You did?"

"I have a little girl now. Samantha. She's five."

Samantha. A good name to say out loud if you haven't used your voice in a while. *Samantha. SA-man-tha. Sa-MAN-tha.*

"Did you ever come back?" I asked. "To check on me?"

"I called until the number was disconnected. She said you were fine."

Fine.

"Does Samantha go to school?" I asked.

He looked at me funny. "Yes. She's in kindergarten."

"How nice for her," I said.

I didn't mean to sound mad. Or maybe I did.

"Your mother said she was homeschooling you."

"My mother barely talked to me."

"I thought you'd be okay."

"I suppose I was. I mean, what's the definition of okay? Satisfactory? I didn't die or anything. And it could have been worse. Look at Anne Frank."

"Look, Bun, I'm sorry. I really am. It's just, when I left, I didn't have a plan. I thought you'd be better off—"

I opened the car door. "Whatever. Just get me some glasses and we'll call it quits."

My legs were like jelly as I walked to the building. *Call it quits?* Who was I and what the bleep was I saying?

He waited outside while the doctor tested my eyes. After, when I was choosing new glasses, the assistant kept saying,

"What do you think, Dad?" and he flinched each time, like he'd stuck a knife in the toaster.

The frames were called tortoiseshell but they reminded me more of my kitten, the one with the brownish-gold fur that got killed by a barbell.

Back in the car he said, "I'd like to take you to Dairy Queen," and I said, "How wonderful, I haven't been there since I was five."

We brought our chocolate-dipped cones to a picnic table.

"There's more I need to say," he said.

I wondered how often he took Samantha for ice cream.

"Then say it," I said. My voice was horrible and nasty, and I actually started to wonder if I was possessed.

I took a lick of my cone.

"This tastes awful."

I dropped it on the ground.

He looked like he might cry again. And I had no *Mustang* to trace.

He stood up and walked slowly to a trash can. He tossed in his cone and paused.

Hurry the hell up.

I don't have all day.

Come back and say what you have to say, you mother-bleeper.

I *was* possessed.

By memories.

Memories of a life without him.

He sat back down, cleared his throat. "The police had a hard time locating me once your mother died. Otherwise I would have come for you straight away."

And what? Taken me to live with Samantha?

Hi. I'm Bernice O'Keefe from Halifax, Nova Scotia. I live with my father in a clean, tidy house. I go to school and have lots of friends. My father, he takes great care of me. I have a sister. She might have freckles too, but I'm not sure 'cause I've never bleepin' met her.

He picked paint flecks off the picnic table with his fingernail.

"I was confused," he said. "When they called, they made no mention of you."

"That's 'cause I didn't exist," I said. "She told everyone I was with you."

"Still. Surely someone would have seen you when they went to collect the body."

"I wasn't even there when she died," I said. "I'd already left 'cause she said, 'Go on! Get out!'"

"But I didn't know that, did I? As far as I knew you were still there. I kept picturing you, alone in that house."

I was *always* alone in that house.

"My head was spinning. I had so many questions. Were you with her when she died? Were you scared?" His voice got thinner and thinner, like he was running out of air. "Were you all alone with a dead body, not knowing what to do?" His sandy colored eyelashes, usually barely there, were dark with dampness. And then he said something that gave me a pang.

"My baby girl," he said, his eyes scanning the whole of my face. "My poor baby girl."

The pang reminded me I was human so I reached out my hand.

He looked at it, but his own didn't budge.

"Relax," I whispered.

His big, freckly fingers wrapped around mine.

"I wasn't sure what to do," he said. "If I told the police, they'd take you into care. They wouldn't give you to me, not after I'd abandoned you once before, not after I left you with her, in that house. So I took off to find you myself. I drove for two days. I thought about you the whole time. And when I got to the house and saw you—oh God, Bun—I was so, so relieved."

"Why didn't you say anything? When you saw me?"

He shrugged. "I was in shock, I guess. I needed time, to think about what to do with you."

"Do with me?"

"Well, I can't leave you here alone, can I?"

"I'm not alone," I said. "I have friends."

He rubbed his thumbs along my fingers. "You're thirteen years old."

I pulled my hand away. "Fourteen."

"Either way you're a minor."

"So?"

"You need to go to school, lead a normal life."

"You suddenly care about me leading a normal life?"

"I'm worried about your future."

"I have a future. I'm going to study hard and someday I'm going to knock the whole world dead."

"I'm sorry, Bun. You can't stay here. Not with a bunch of twenty-year-olds."

"Then why did you say you'd pay our rent?"

"I need time, to go back to Halifax, to sort a few things out."

A lightbulb went on in my head. "They don't know about me, do they?"

"I didn't want to complicate things."

"So why start now?"

"Things have changed."

"They won't like me, you know."

"They'll learn to."

"They'll look at me funny, just like you do."

He opened his mouth but nothing came out.

"I won't fit in and you know it."

I gave him time to disagree.

I knew he wouldn't.

"If you take me away," I said, "you'll ruin both our lives. I've never asked you for anything. I just want this one thing. I want to stay."

He looked at me, all over my face, back and forth and all around.

"Those people you live with," he said. "They treat you good?"

"Yes. They filled up my insides. They peeled back my layers and taught me how to feel. They told me stories and called me 'my ducky.' They fed me till my pants got tight. They laughed at jokes I never made. They said, 'I like you, Bun O'Keefe,' and helped me breathe again."

My words were his escape route.

"You're going to be fine, aren't you?"

I gave him the answer he wanted to hear. Luckily, it was the truth.

"Yes."

"I'll miss you, Bun."

In a weird way, I knew that was the truth too.

He took my hand.

"I'm going to be checking up on you, you know. Phone calls. Pop visits."

He liked wearing his Dad hat. Too bad it didn't fit him right.

"I'll pay for the house, as long as you need it. Food, clothes, whatever. All you have to do is ask."

I didn't want to talk anymore. "Can I have another chocolate-dipped cone?"

He told me about Samantha while we ate. She had lots of

friends and a great sense of humor. It gave me this weird feeling. Like I was shrinking.

He pointed at his watch. "We'd better go or I'll be in big trouble." And then he imitated Busker Boy's chest-rumbling voice. "Two. Hours."

I said, "You'd better watch out. He almost killed a man once." And then I added, "Just kidding," in case he believed me.

On the way home I sang the song he used to sing about love being strange. I said, "It's okay that you quit; I forgive you."

"Bun, I—"

"She would have quit, too, if she could have. 'Cause I'm a strange alien being. But she didn't have a chance 'cause you left first."

He took his eyes off the road, just for a second, to look at me. "Is that what she made you think? That I left because of you?"

"She told me I was retarded."

His gripped the wheel. "Jesus Christ."

"Don't worry," I said. "I didn't believe her."

He glanced at me again. "I left because of her, not you. I can promise you that."

I wondered if he was faithful, like Horton.

When we pulled up to the house, with its gables and moldings and fancy trim, he said, "You look real smart in

those glasses, Bunny," and I said, "Thanks, thanks a lot."
Then I shut the door of his pride and joy and ran inside to
my constant.

~

He was relaxing on the couch, reading, but when I squeezed
in next to him I could feel the thump of his heart.

He laid his book on his chest. "Well?"

"I felt like I was shrinking at one point."

He turned on his side to make room. "Shrinking?"

"Yeah. But I'm back to normal now."

"So everything's okay?"

"Yes. Everything's really clear now."

"I like them a lot," he said.

"Like what?"

"Your glasses."

I reached up and touched the kitten-fur frames. "He said
they make me look smart."

"You are smart."

"I have lots to tell you. But not now, okay?"

"Okay."

I closed my eyes and listened to his breathing, waiting for
the spark to burst.

~

I crouched near the stream collecting stones.

Busker Boy played his guitar. He stared into the distance, and I wondered if he was thinking about going back to his community, and I wondered, too, if white people could live there 'cause I knew he wouldn't go there without me.

I had three stones in my hand. One for Busker Boy, one for Big Eyes and one for Chef. A shiny stone glistened from under the water. I lost my balance reaching for it.

"Be careful," said Busker Boy. "That water is cold."

I caught myself and said, "I'm all right don't worry about me, don't worry. I'm all right," and he smiled 'cause we'd watched Jimmy Quinlan together and he knew I was doing Arthur O'Malley.

He sang a song about dreams coming true if you want them to. I liked that.

We stayed for ages and when it got dark we walked back through the trees. It was a damp and dirty spring but I could see a silver lining—everything was melting and soon there'd be color all around us. I showed him the stone I'd chosen for him. I said, "It'd be heart-shaped if it weren't for this dent in the bottom." He reached out, ran his finger along the edge. "It's perfect."

The brown grass crunched under our feet and it was like the beat for our walk and when the ground beneath us became a tangle of overgrown shrubbery and fallen branches Busker Boy said, "Take my hand, Nishim."

So I did.

The End

ACKNOWLEDGEMENTS

Many thanks to my agent, Amy Tompkins, for embracing this story, and to my editor, Lynne Missen, for strengthening it. Thanks also to the Ontario Arts Council for their generous funding; to Duncan and Rosie for their generous feedback; and to John W. Smith for his belief in me as a writer. To April, although you are too young to read Bun's story, your blind admiration keeps me motivated. Finally, special thanks to Innu artist Mary Ann Penashue for her steadfast support of this work. In the immortal words of Bun O'Keefe, "Thank you, thanks a lot, wow, thanks."